10/04
14.95

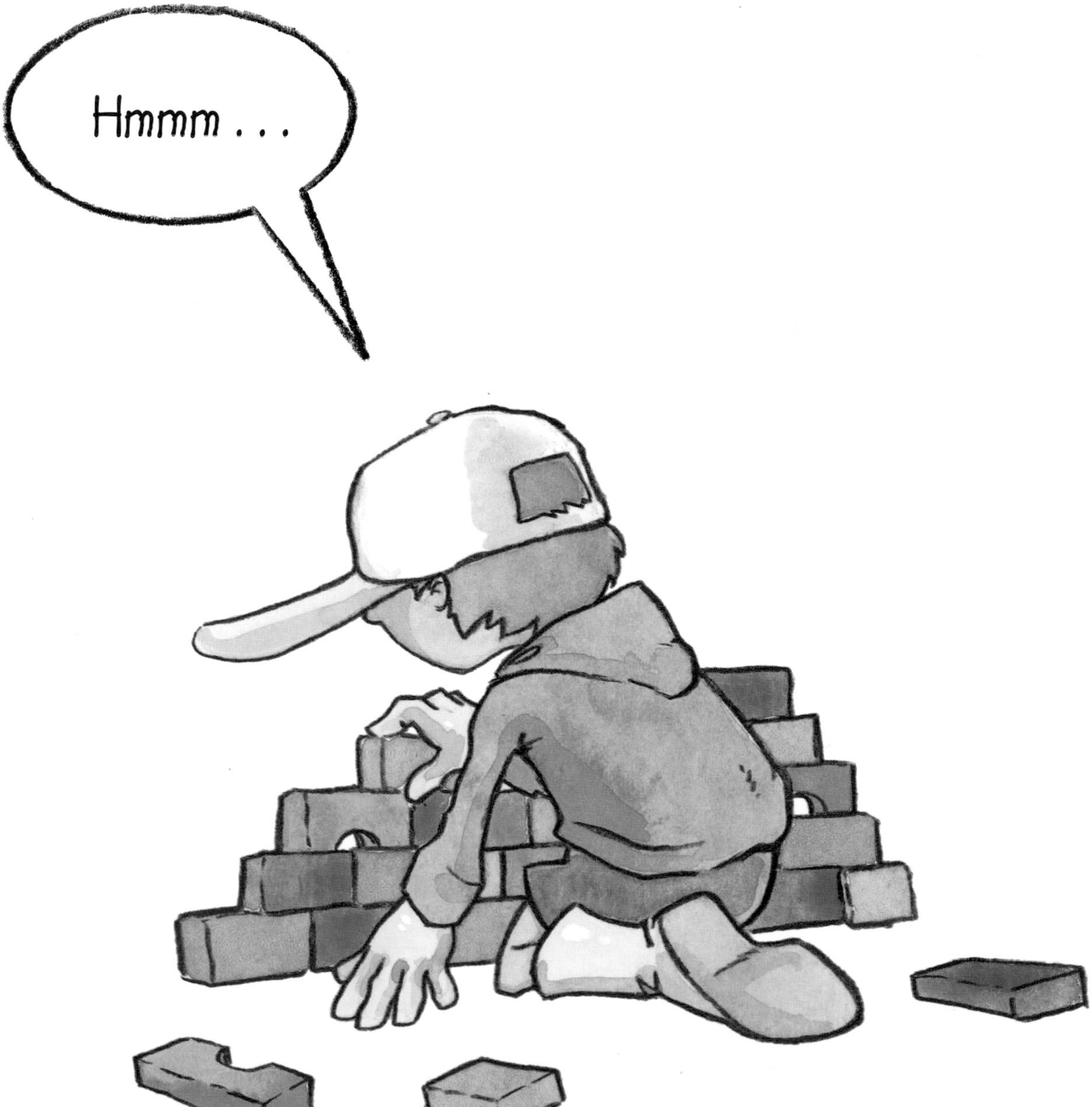
Hmmm . . .

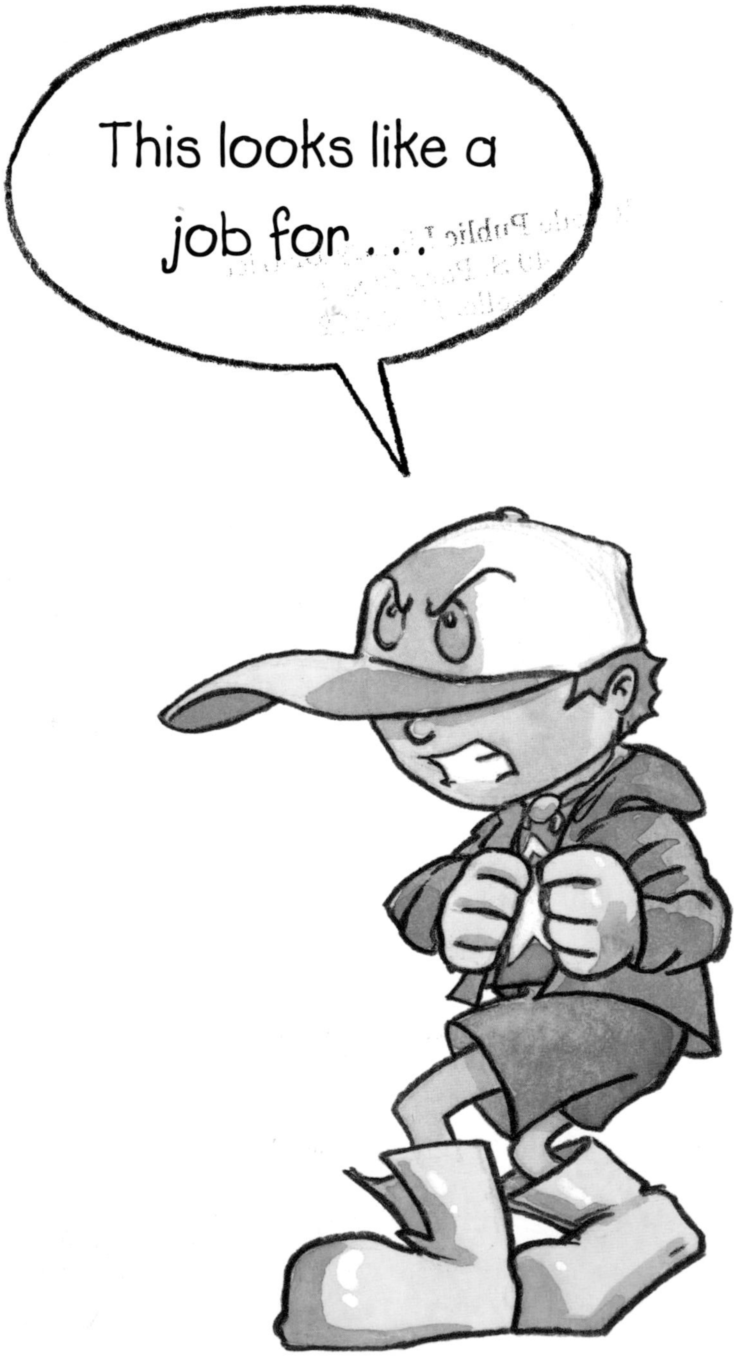
This looks like a job for . . .

Simon & Schuster Books for Young Readers
New York London Toronto Sydney

# KAPOW!



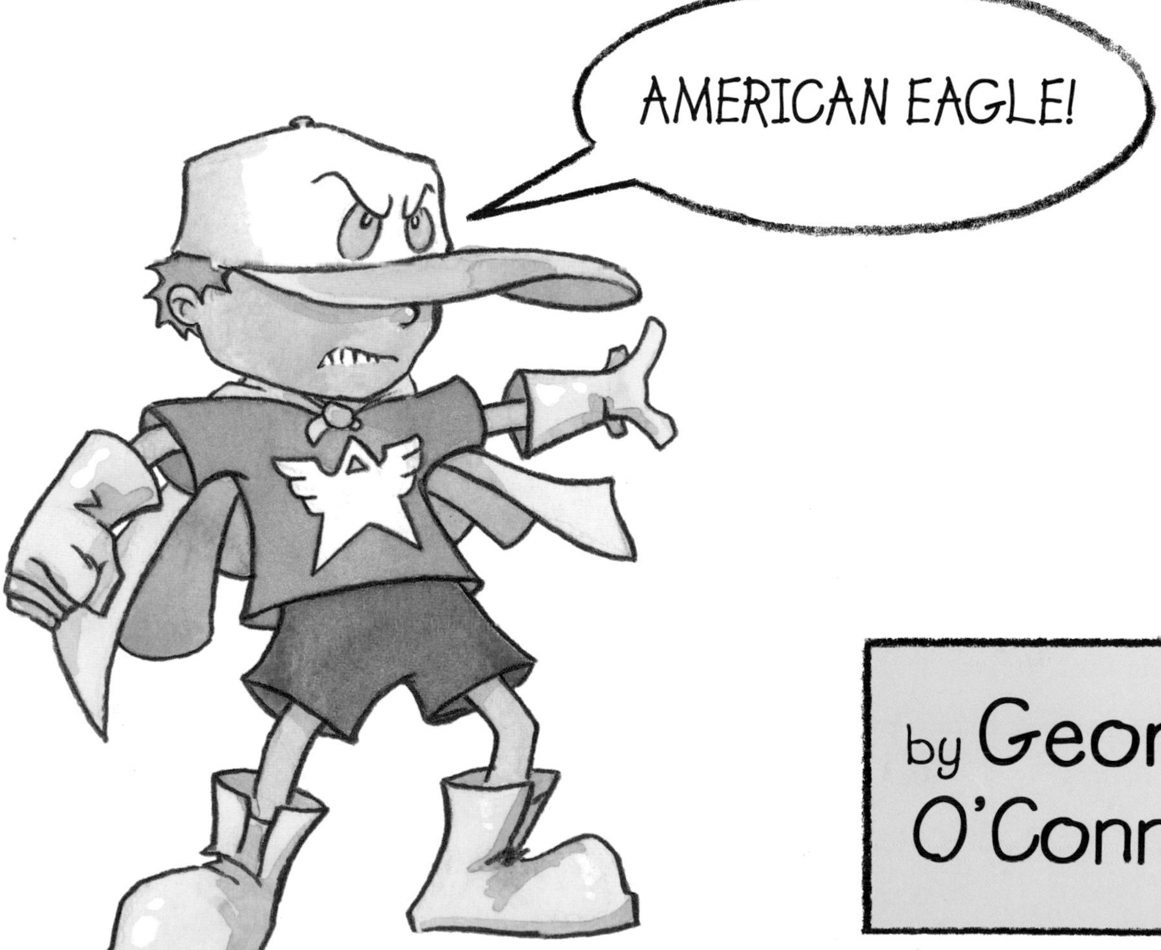
AMERICAN EAGLE!

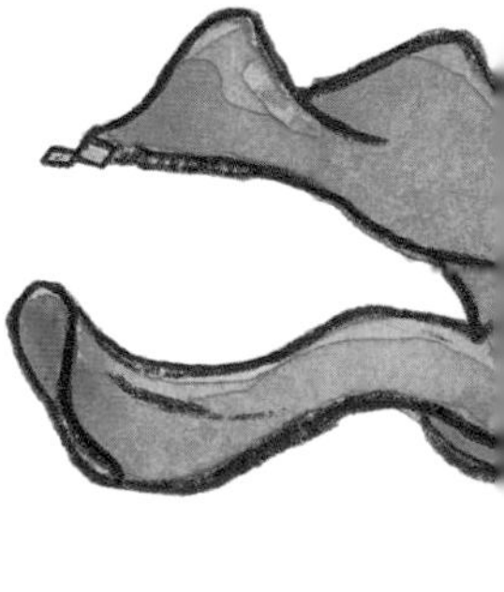

by George O'Connor

SIMON & SCHUSTER BOOKS FOR YOUNG READERS
An imprint of Simon & Schuster Children's Publishing Division
1230 Avenue of the Americas, New York, New York 10020
Copyright © 2004 by George O'Connor
All rights reserved, including the right of reproduction in whole or
in part in any form.
SIMON & SCHUSTER BOOKS FOR YOUNG READERS is a trademark of
Simon & Schuster, Inc.

Library of Congress
Cataloging-in-Publication Data
O'Connor, George.
Kapow! / [written and illustrated by]
George O'Connor.—1st ed.
p. cm.
Summary: Truth, justice, and the American Eagle way! A young boy realizes what
it really means to be a superhero.
ISBN 0-689-86718-2
[1. Play—Fiction.] I. Title.
PZ7.O22185 Kap 2004
[E]—dc21                2003009354

Book design by Mark Siegel
The text for this book is set in Lemonade.
The illustrations for this book are rendered in
black pencil, watercolors, and acrylics.
Manufactured in China
10 9 8 7 6 5 4 3 2

first edition

To Stan, Jack, Joe, Steve, and Bill

–G. O.

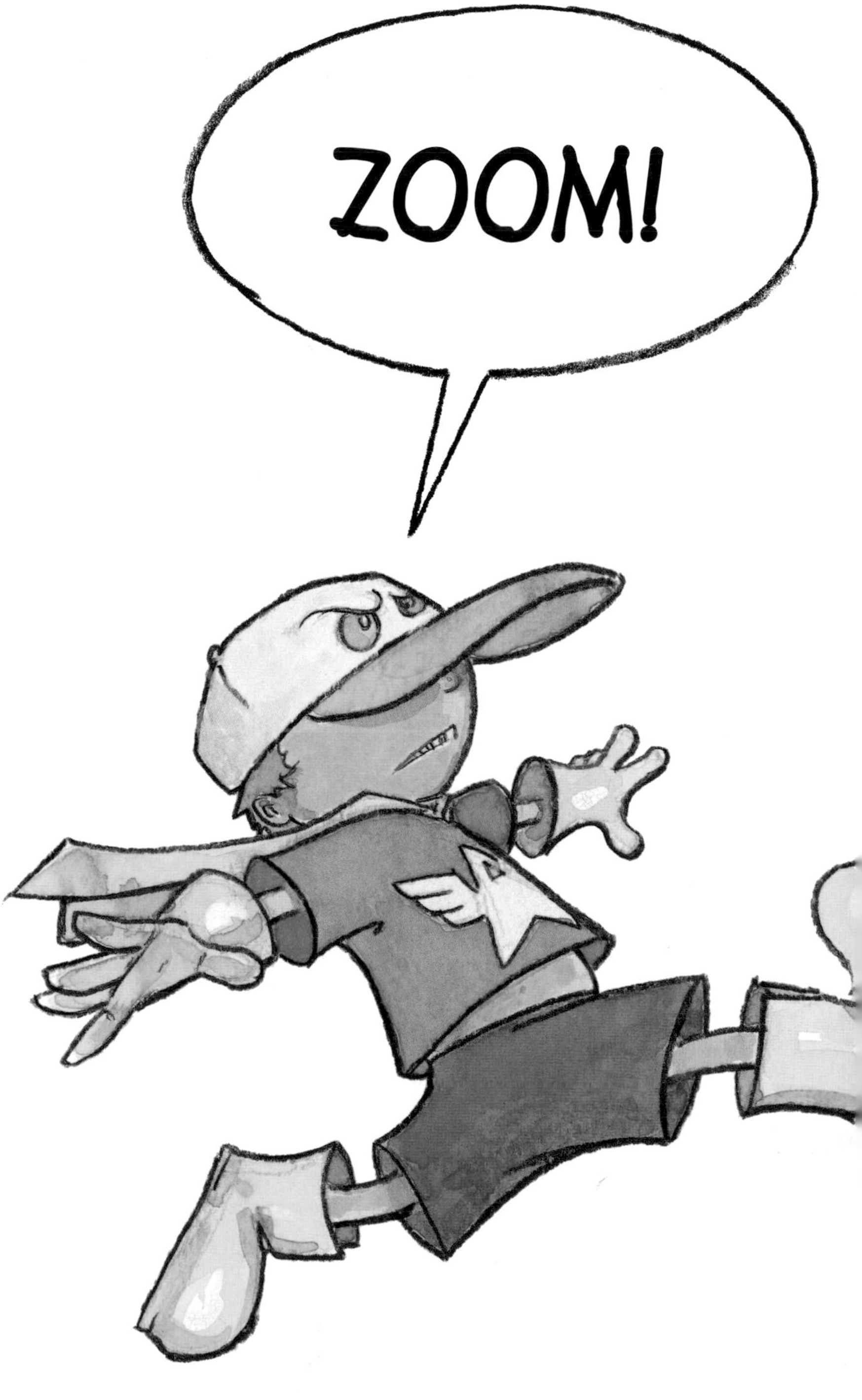
ZOOM!

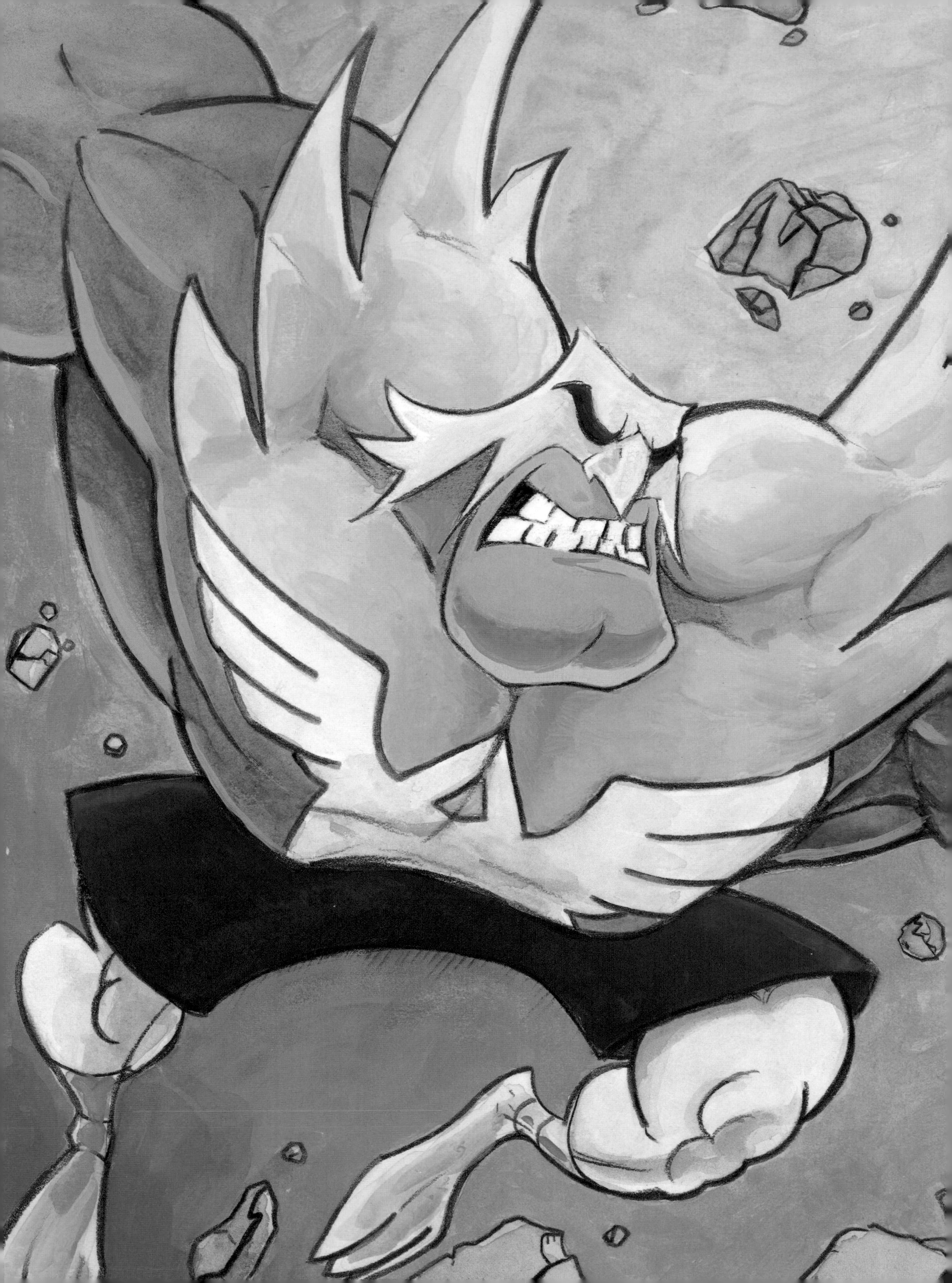

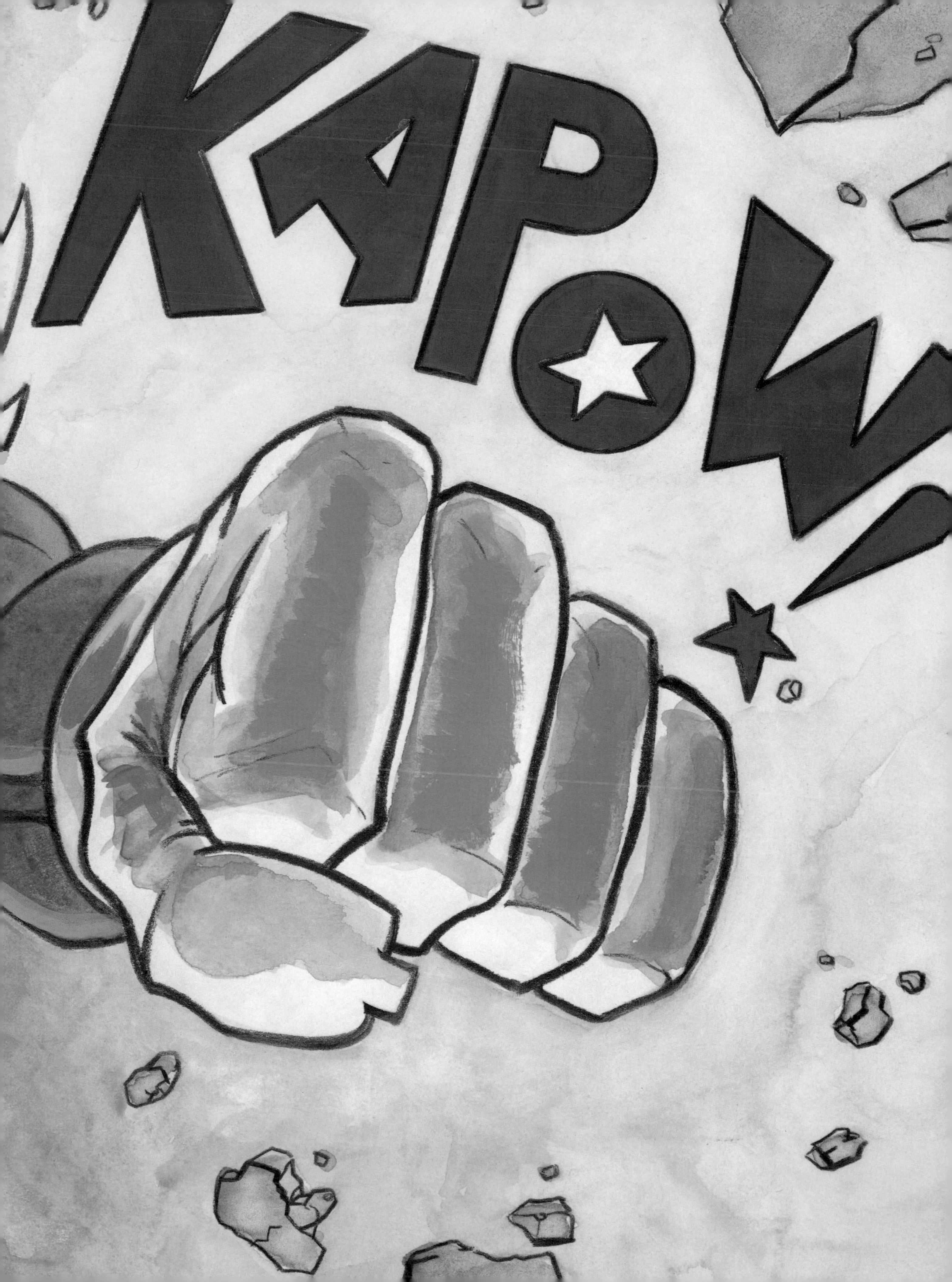
KAPOW!

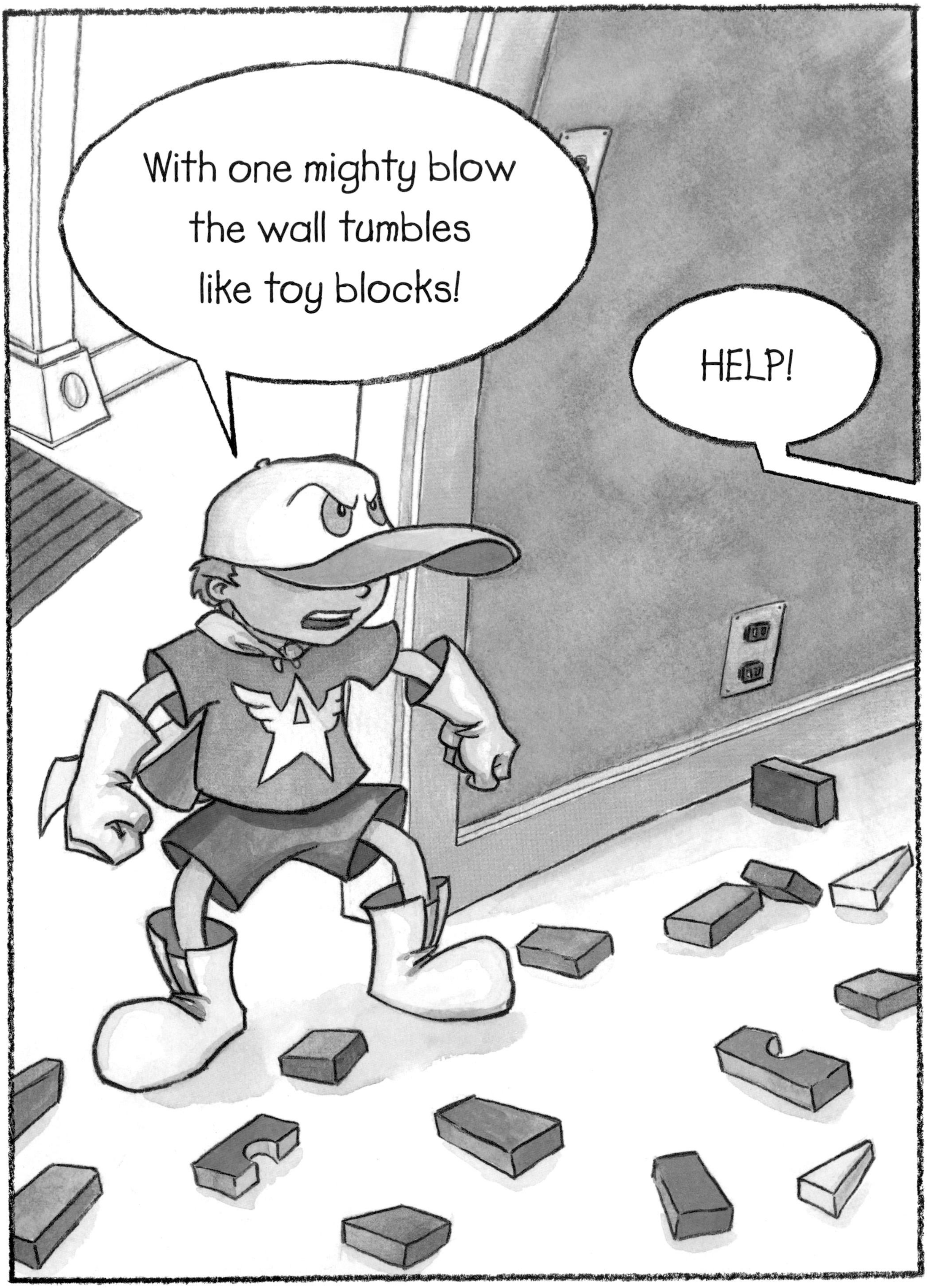
With one mighty blow the wall tumbles like toy blocks!
HELP!

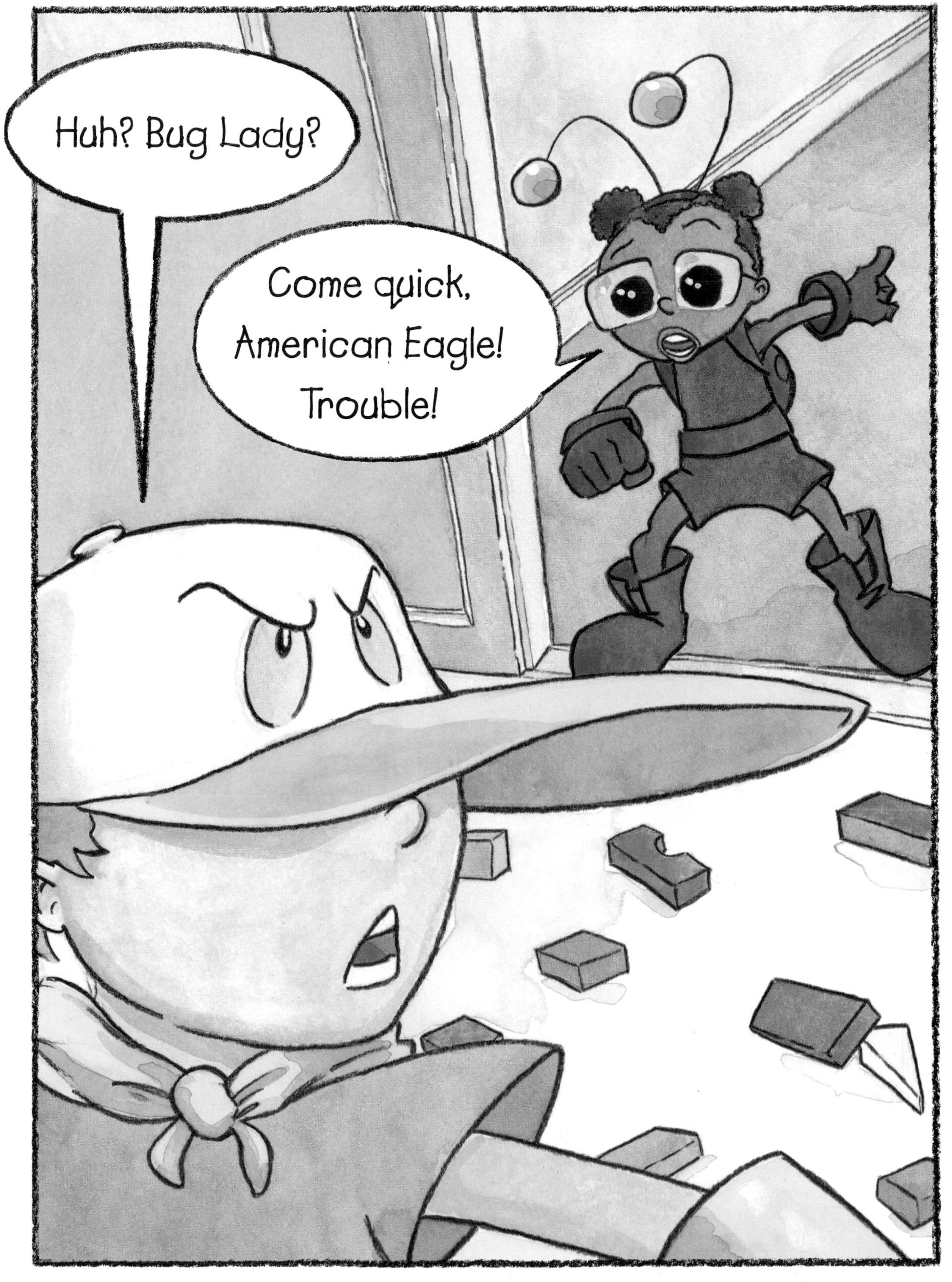
Huh? Bug Lady?
Come quick, American Eagle! Trouble!

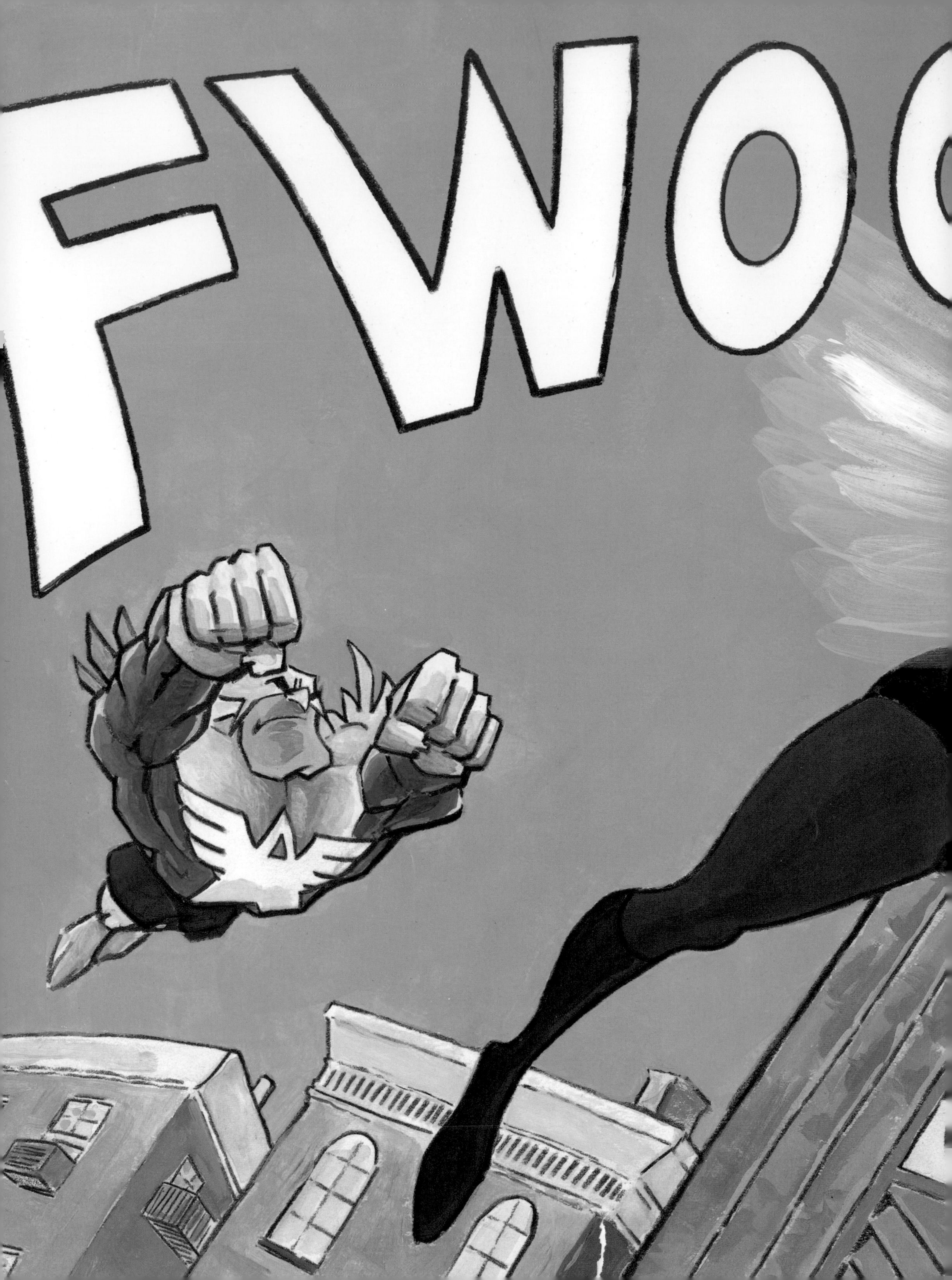
FWO

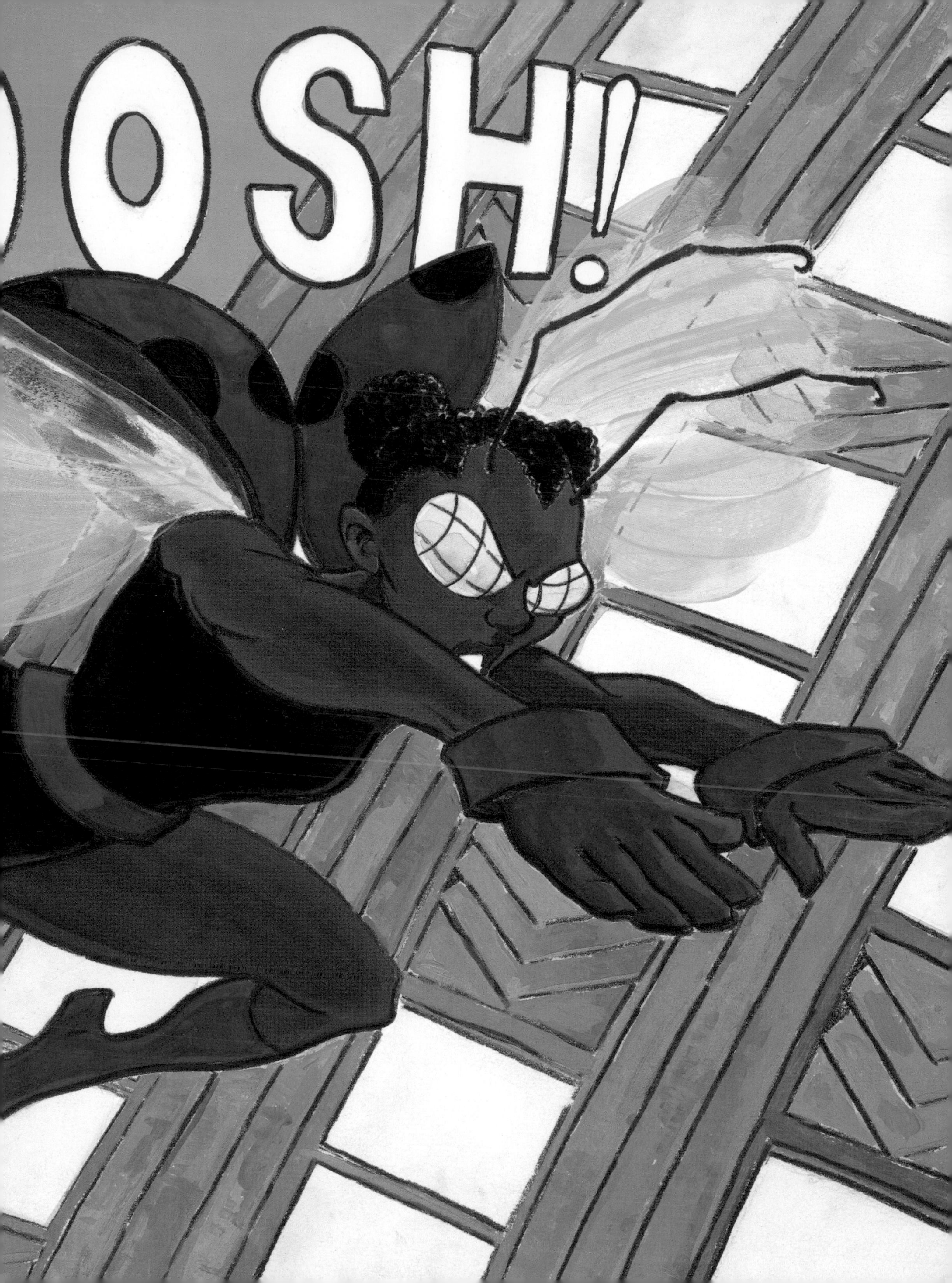
OOSH!

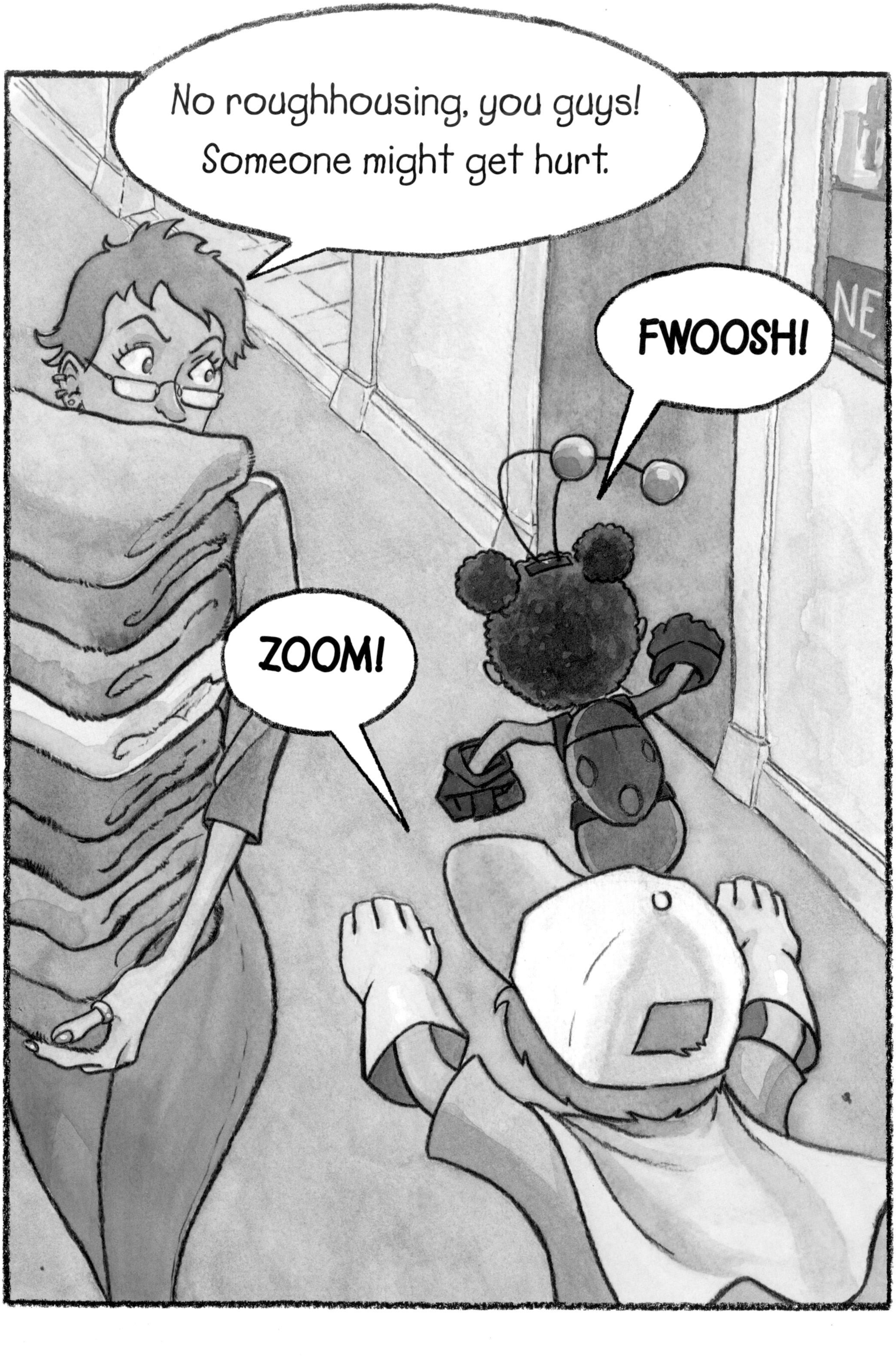
No roughhousing, you guys! Someone might get hurt.
FWOOSH!
ZOOM!

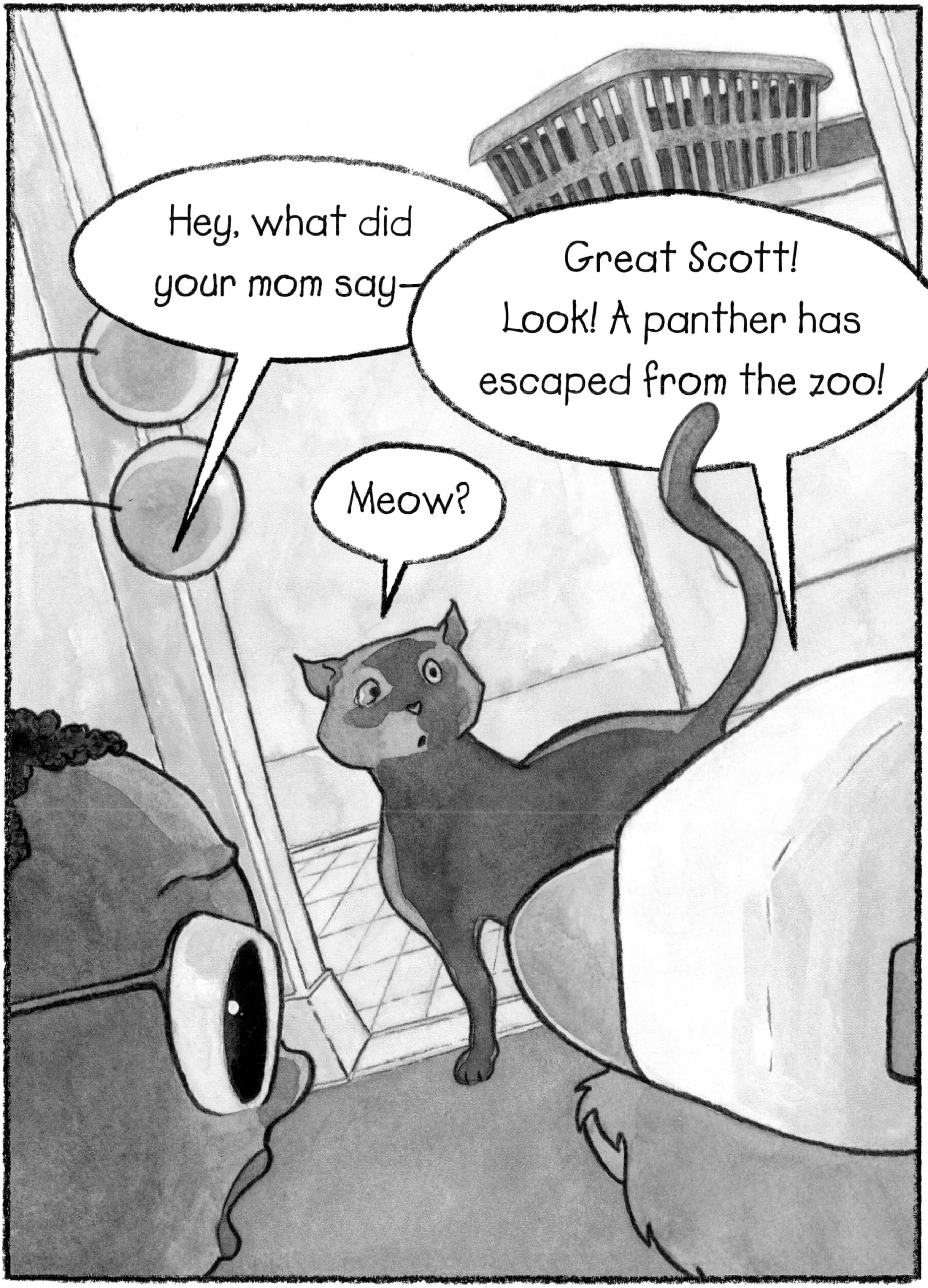
Hey, what did your mom say—
Great Scott! Look! A panther has escaped from the zoo!
Meow?

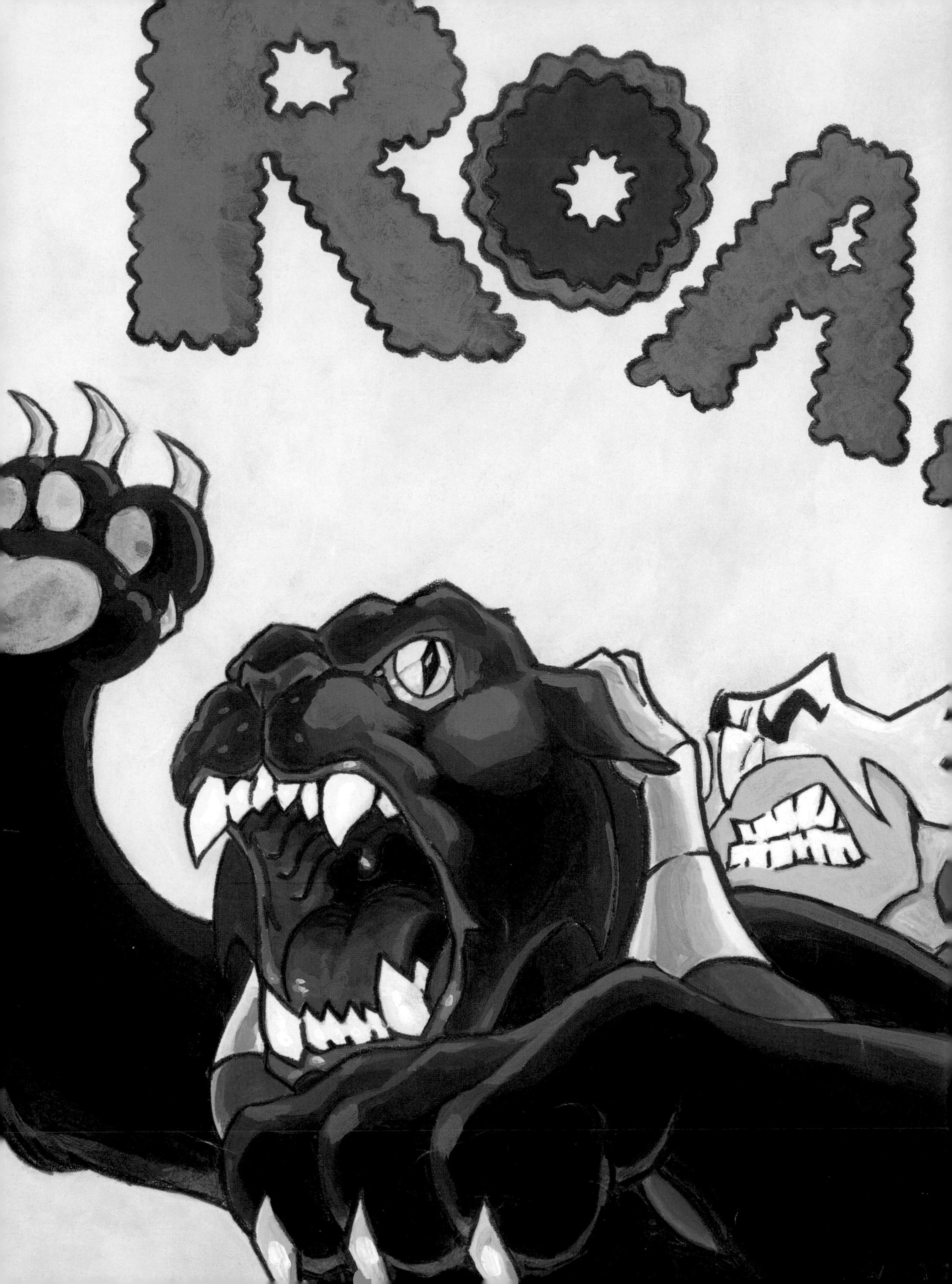
ROA

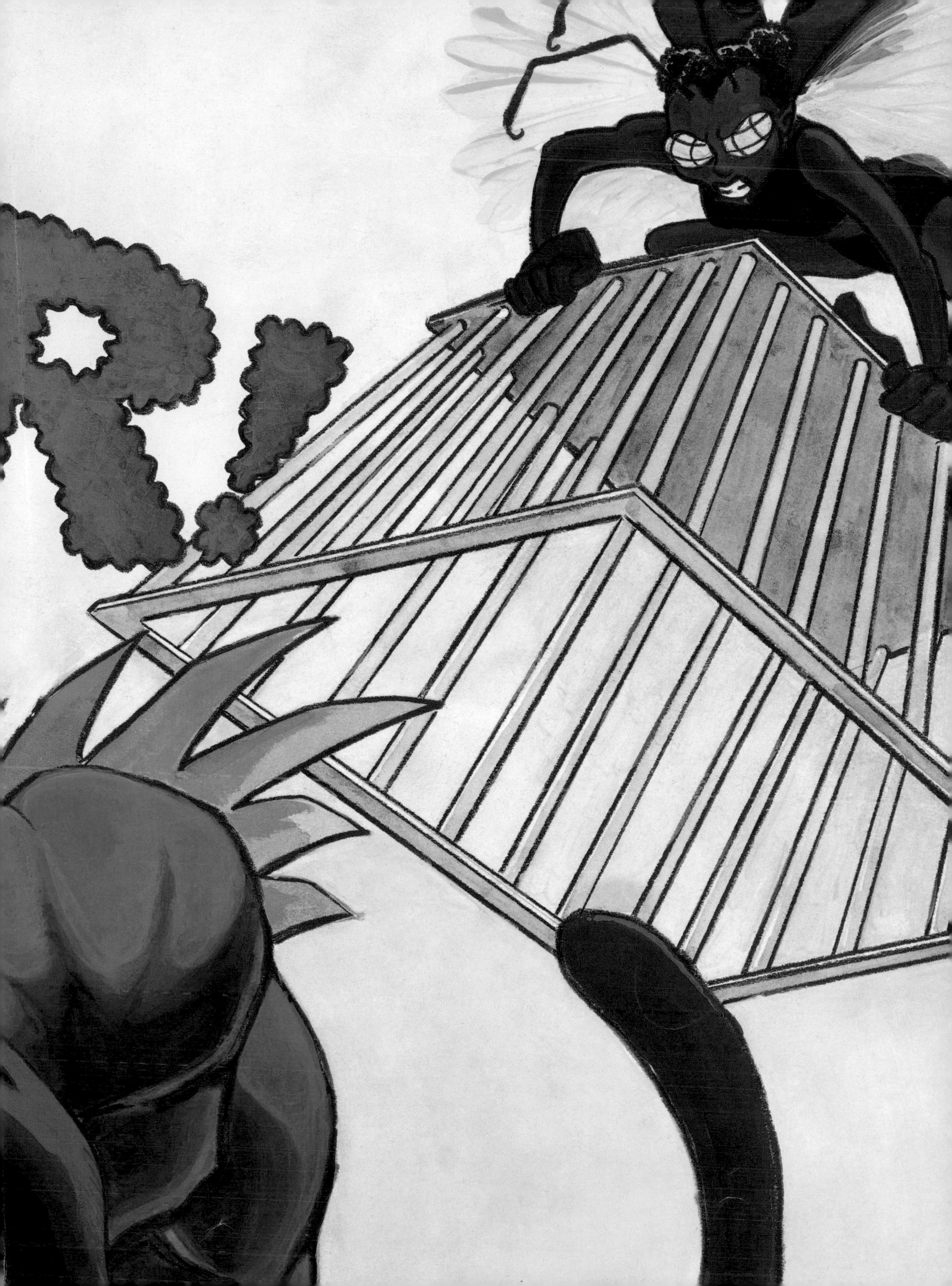

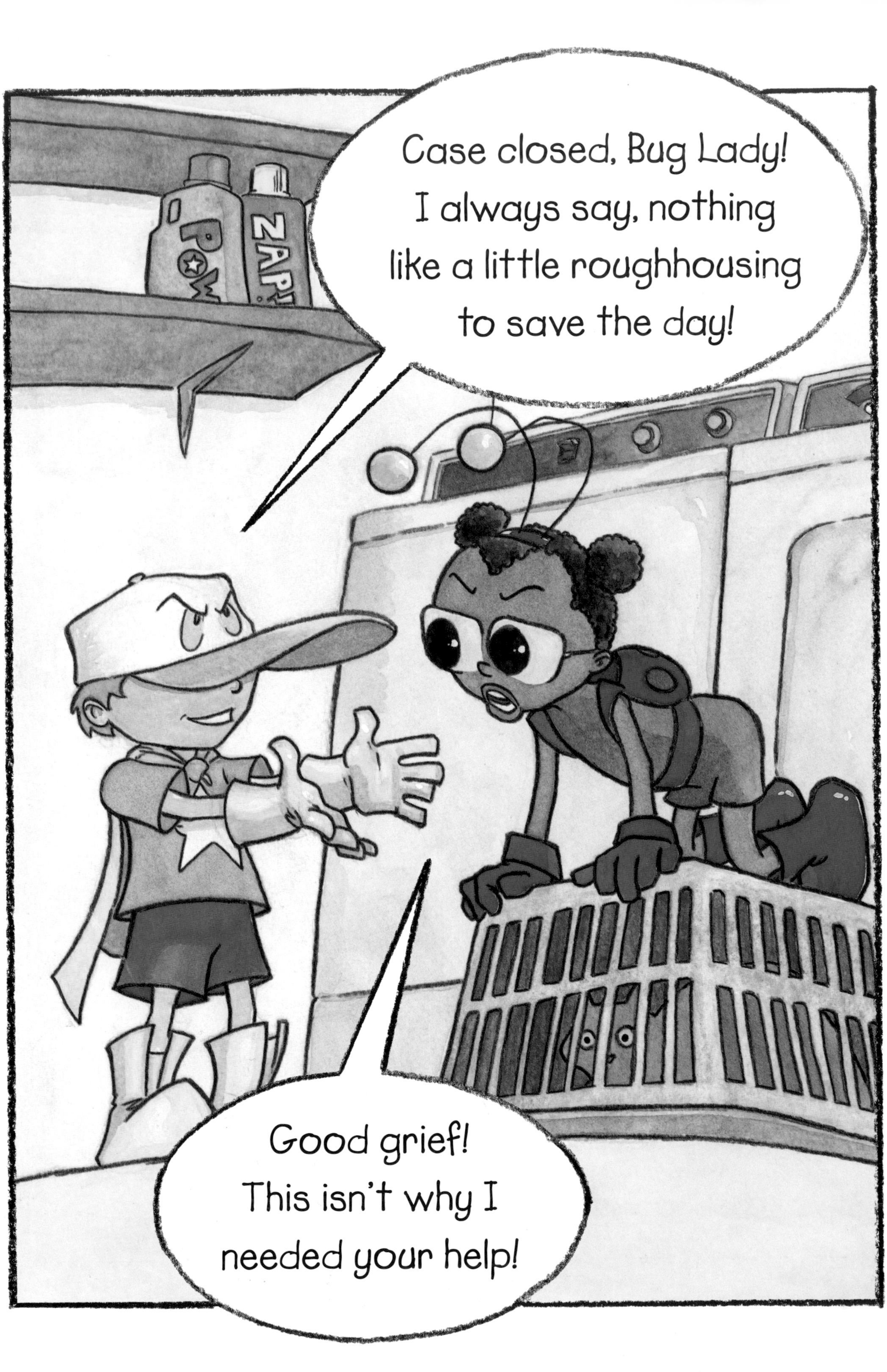
Case closed, Bug Lady! I always say, nothing like a little roughhousing to save the day!
POW
ZAP
Good grief! This isn't why I needed your help!

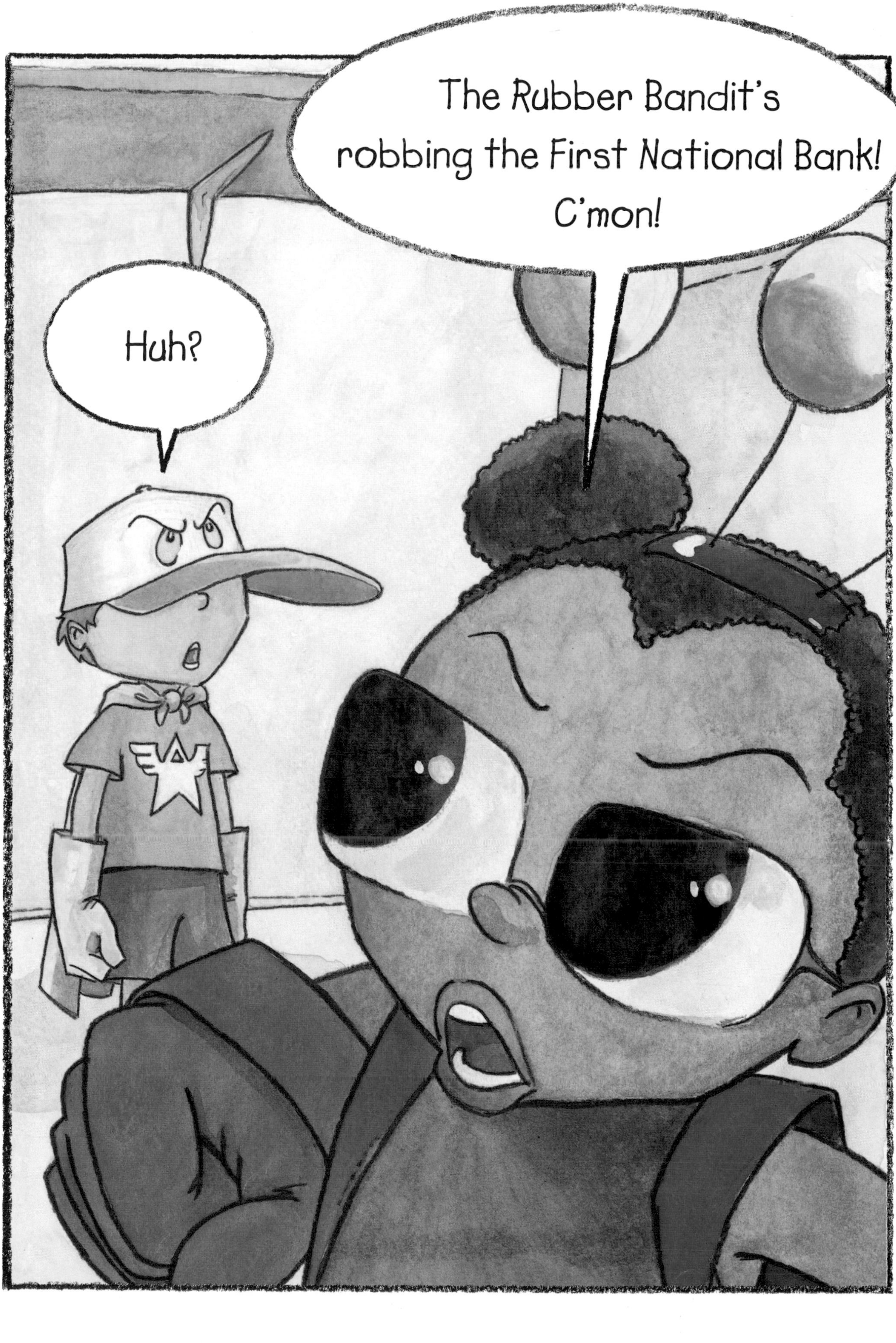
Huh?
The Rubber Bandit's robbing the First National Bank! C'mon!

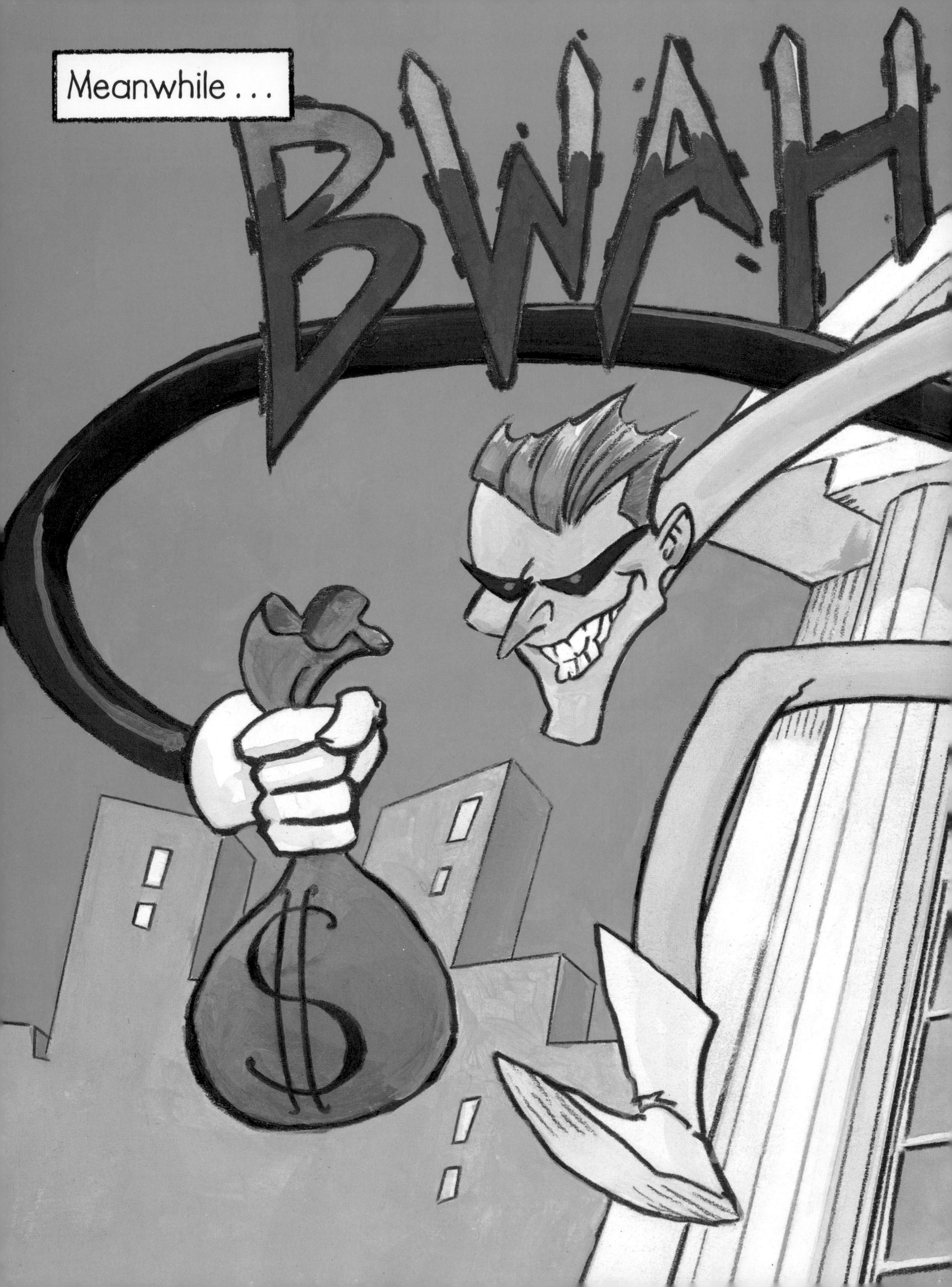
Meanwhile . . .
BWAH

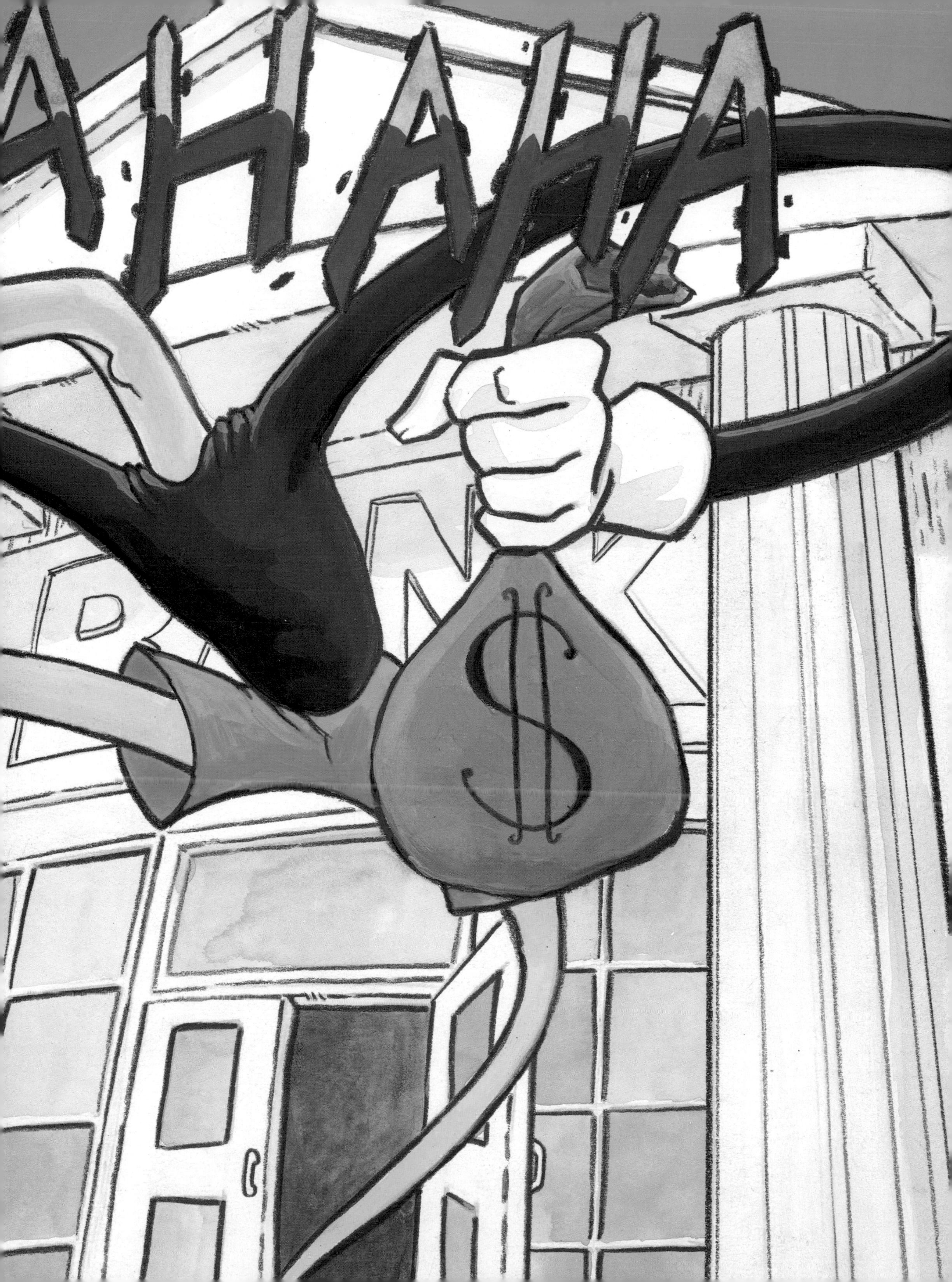
AHAHA

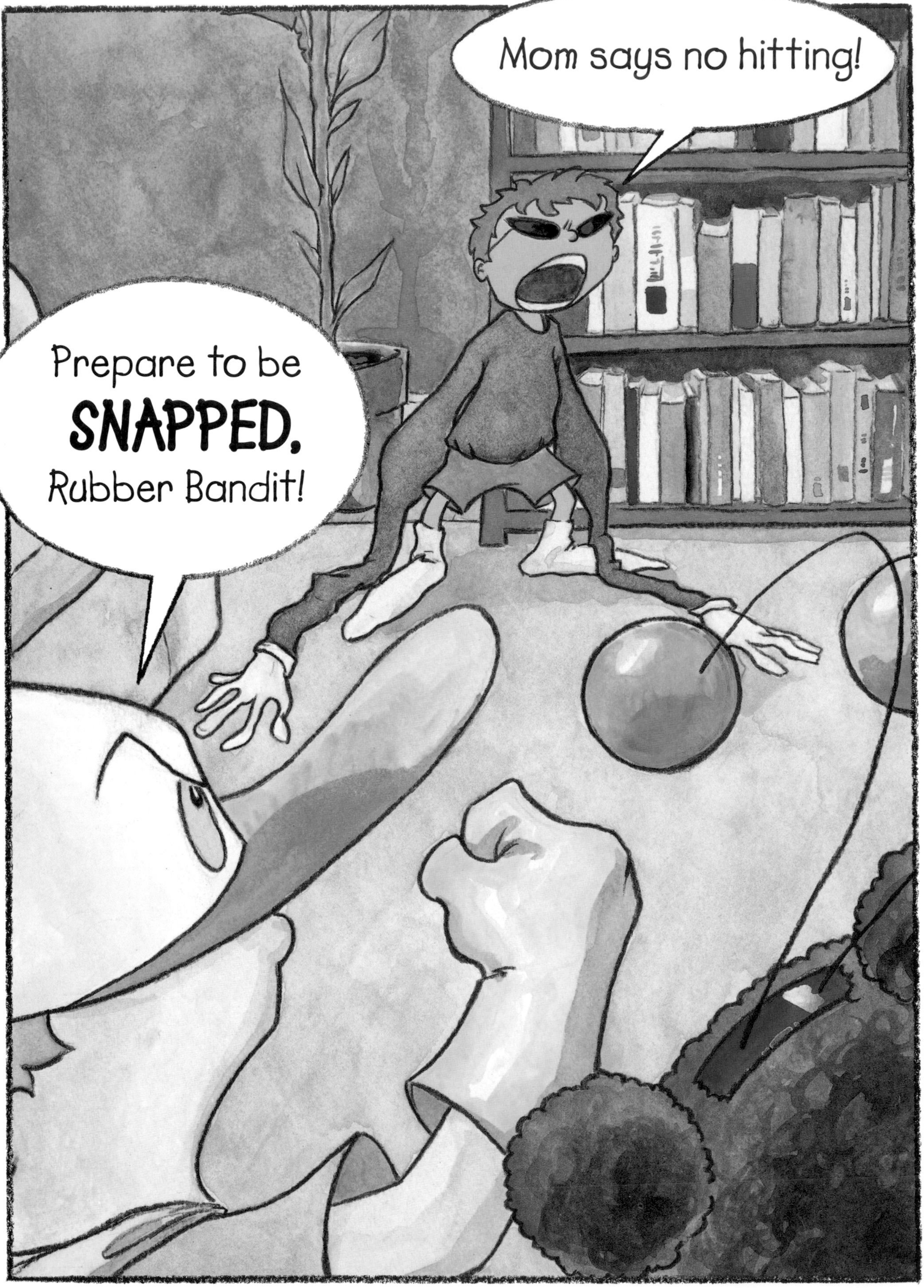
Mom says no hitting!
Prepare to be SNAPPED, Rubber Bandit!

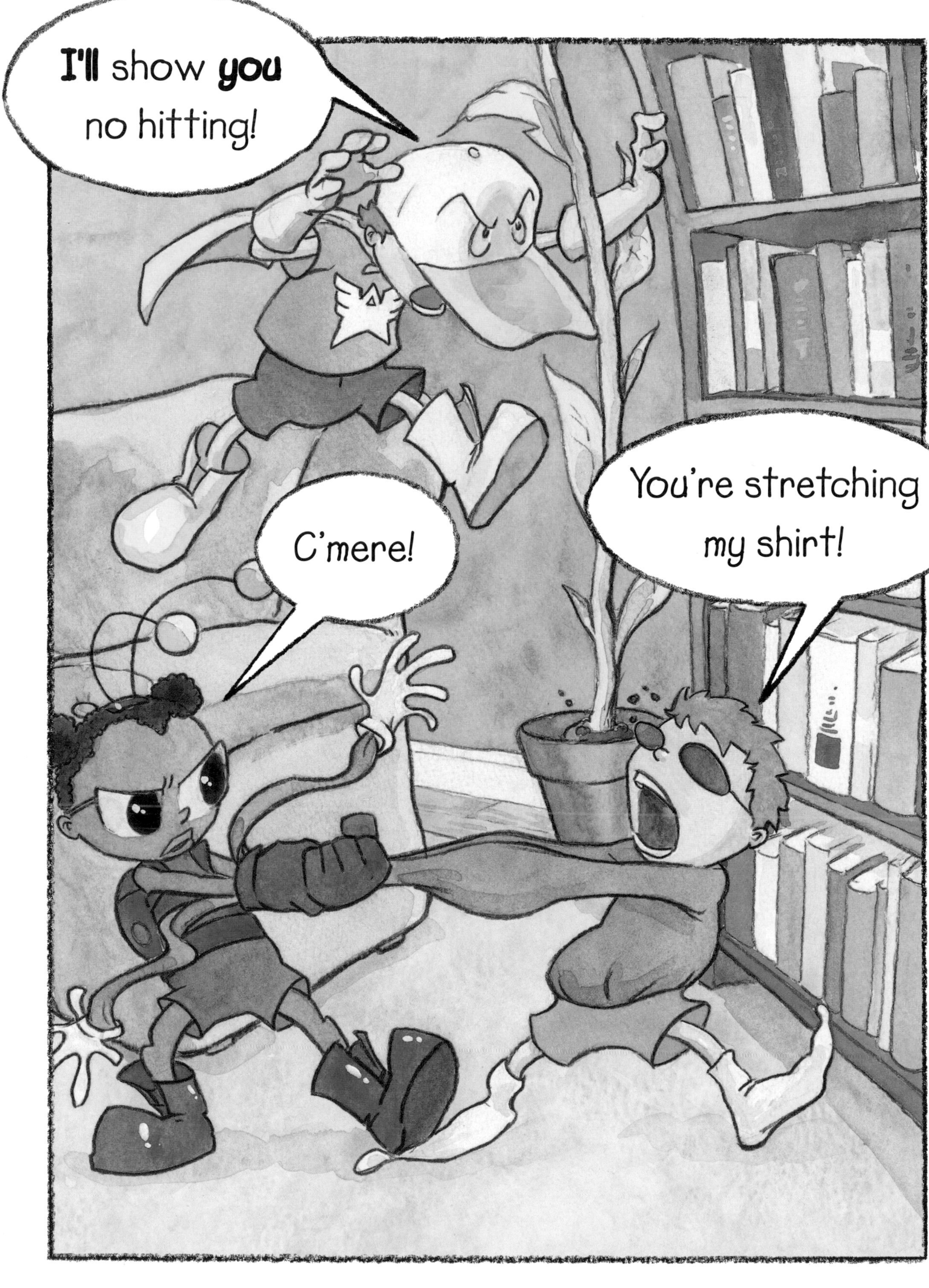
**I'll** show ***you*** no hitting!
C'mere!
You're stretching my shirt!

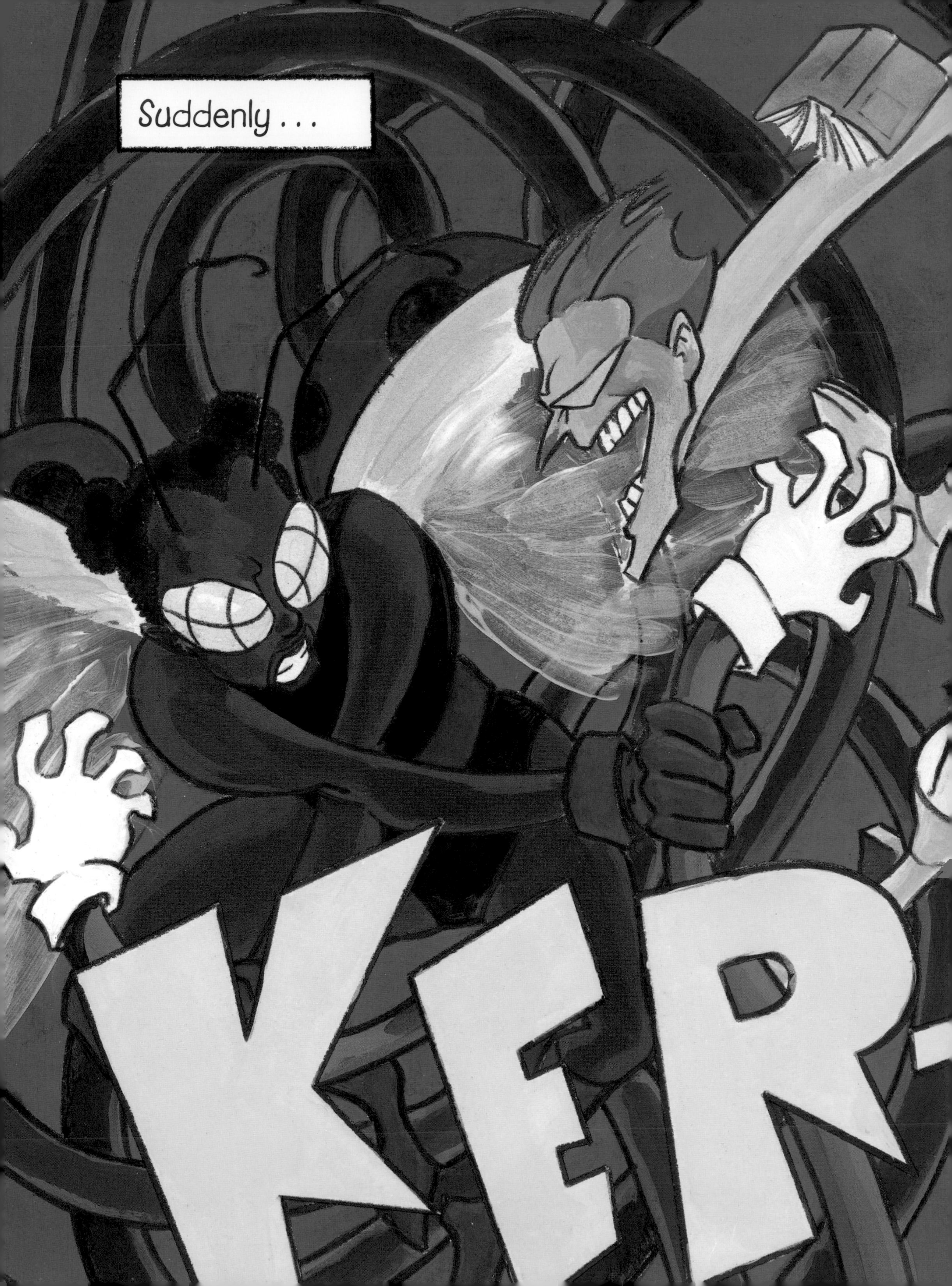
Suddenly . . .
KER-

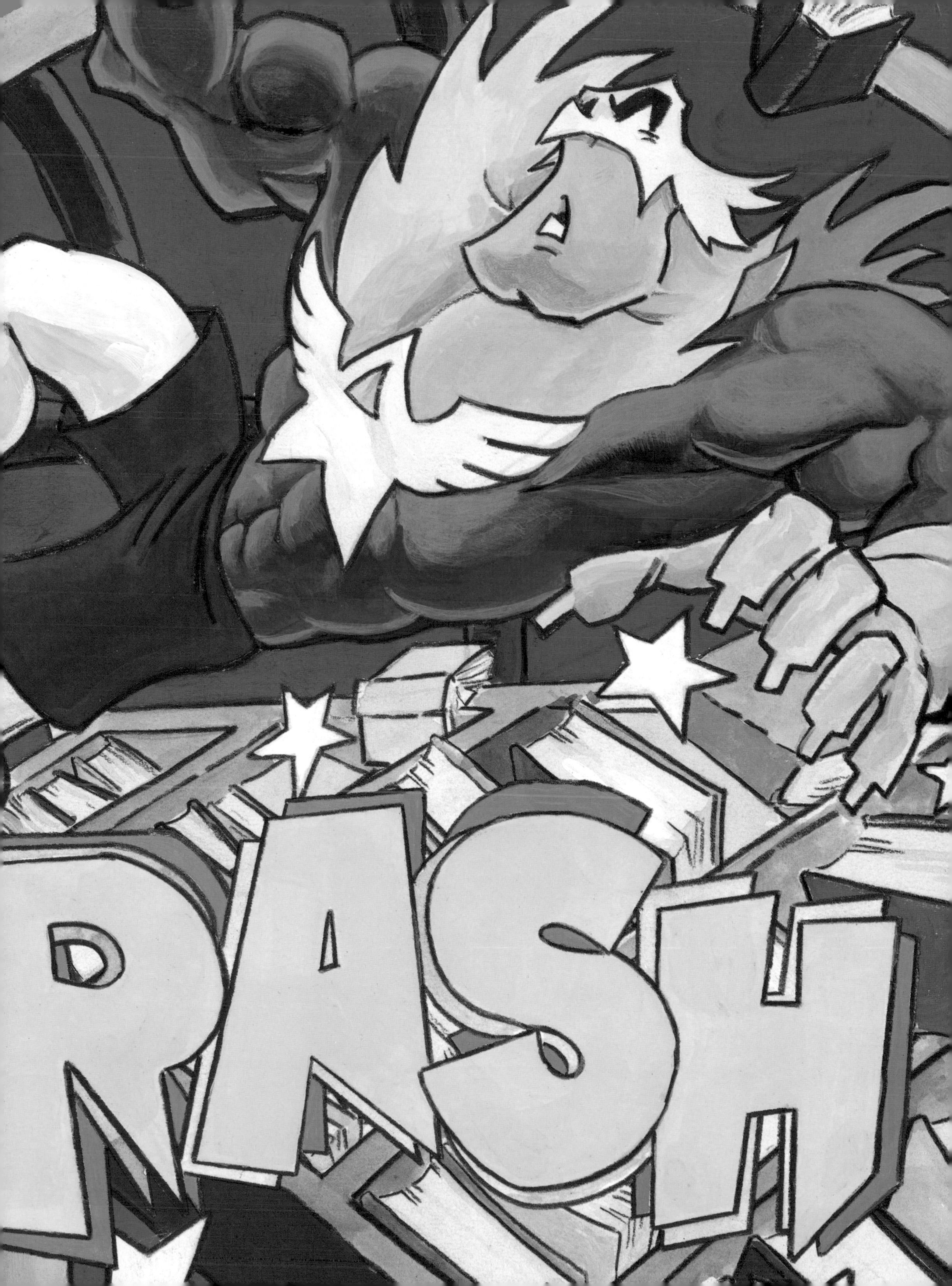
RASH

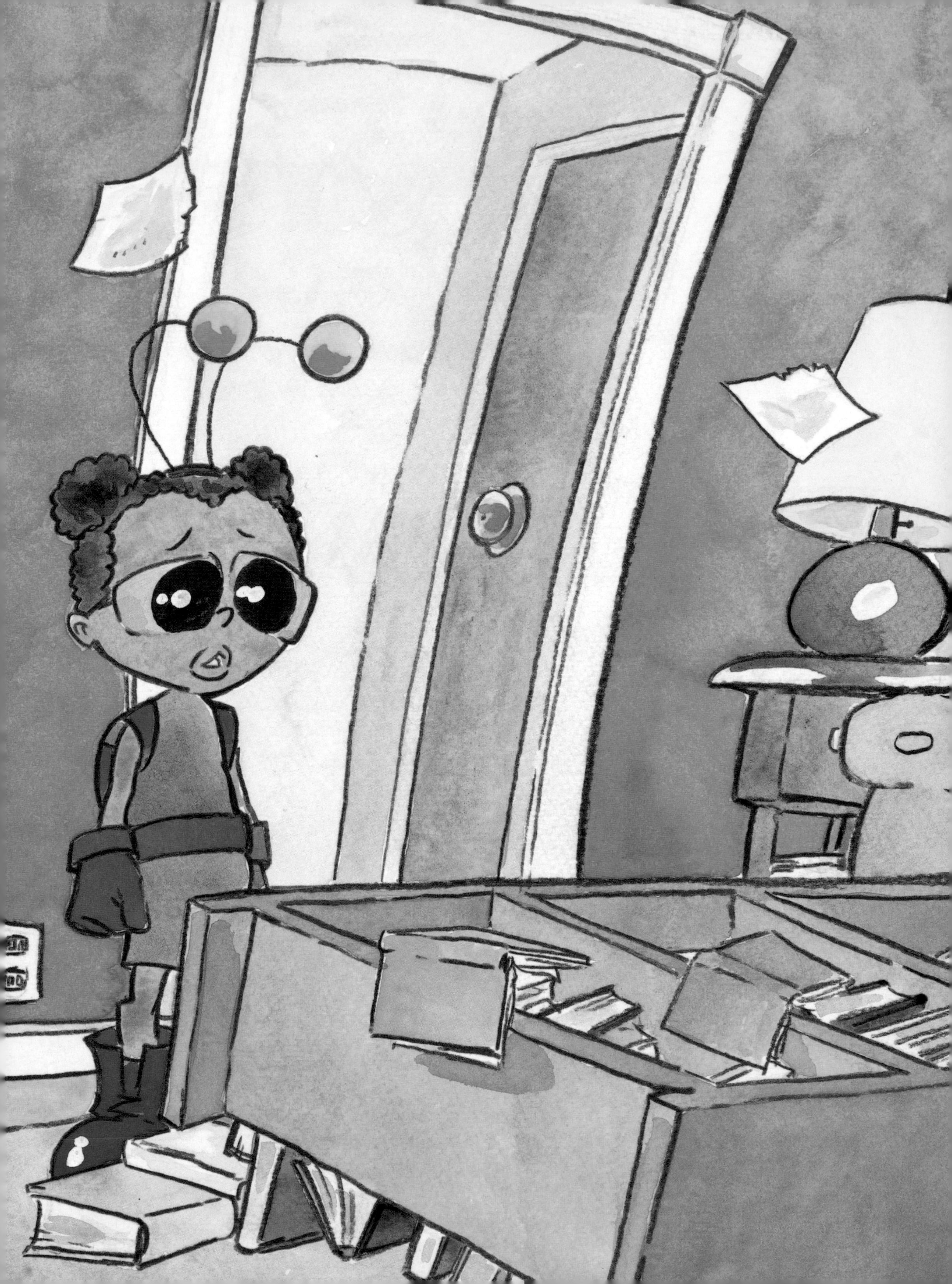

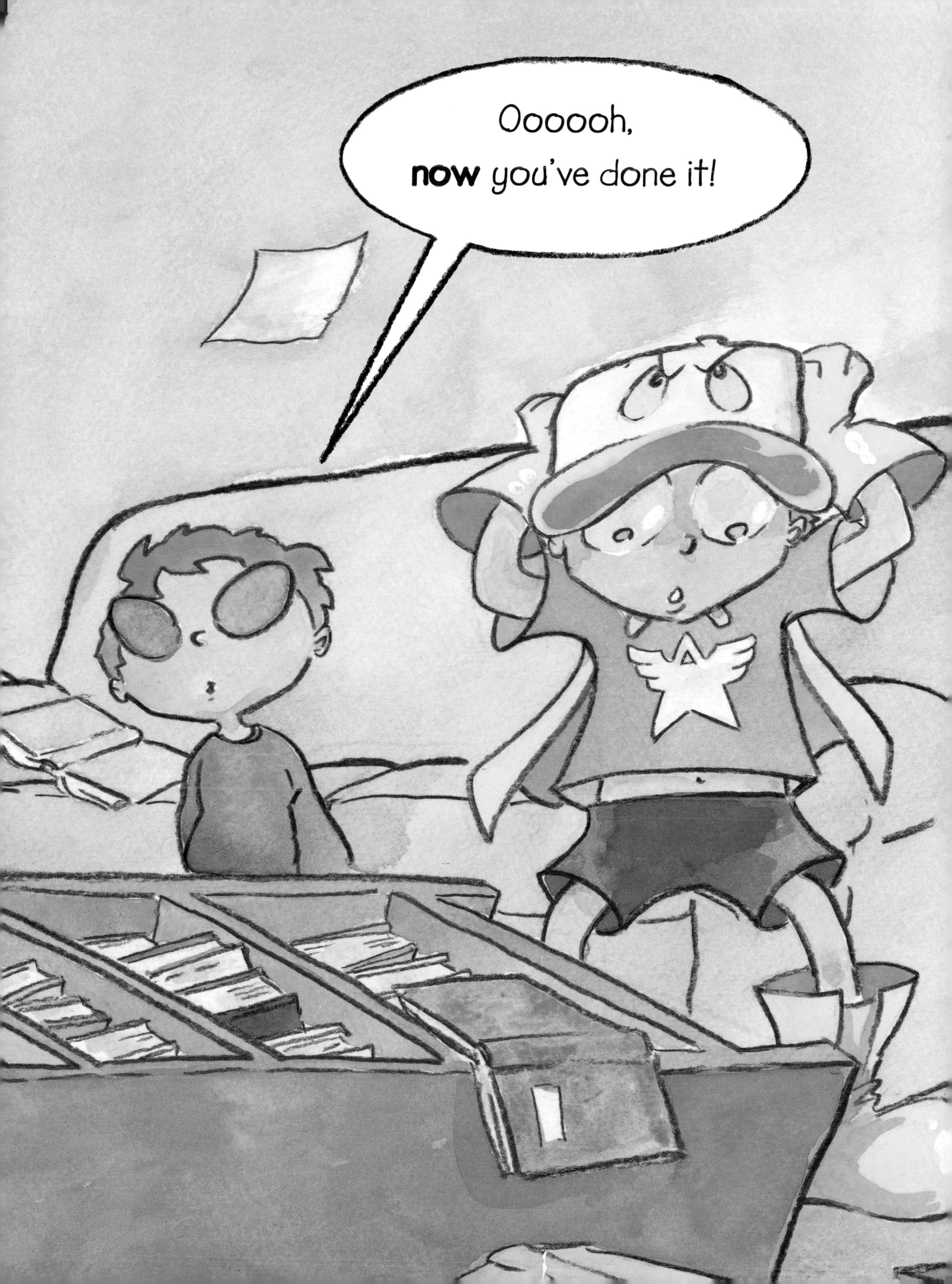
Oooooh, **now** you've done it!

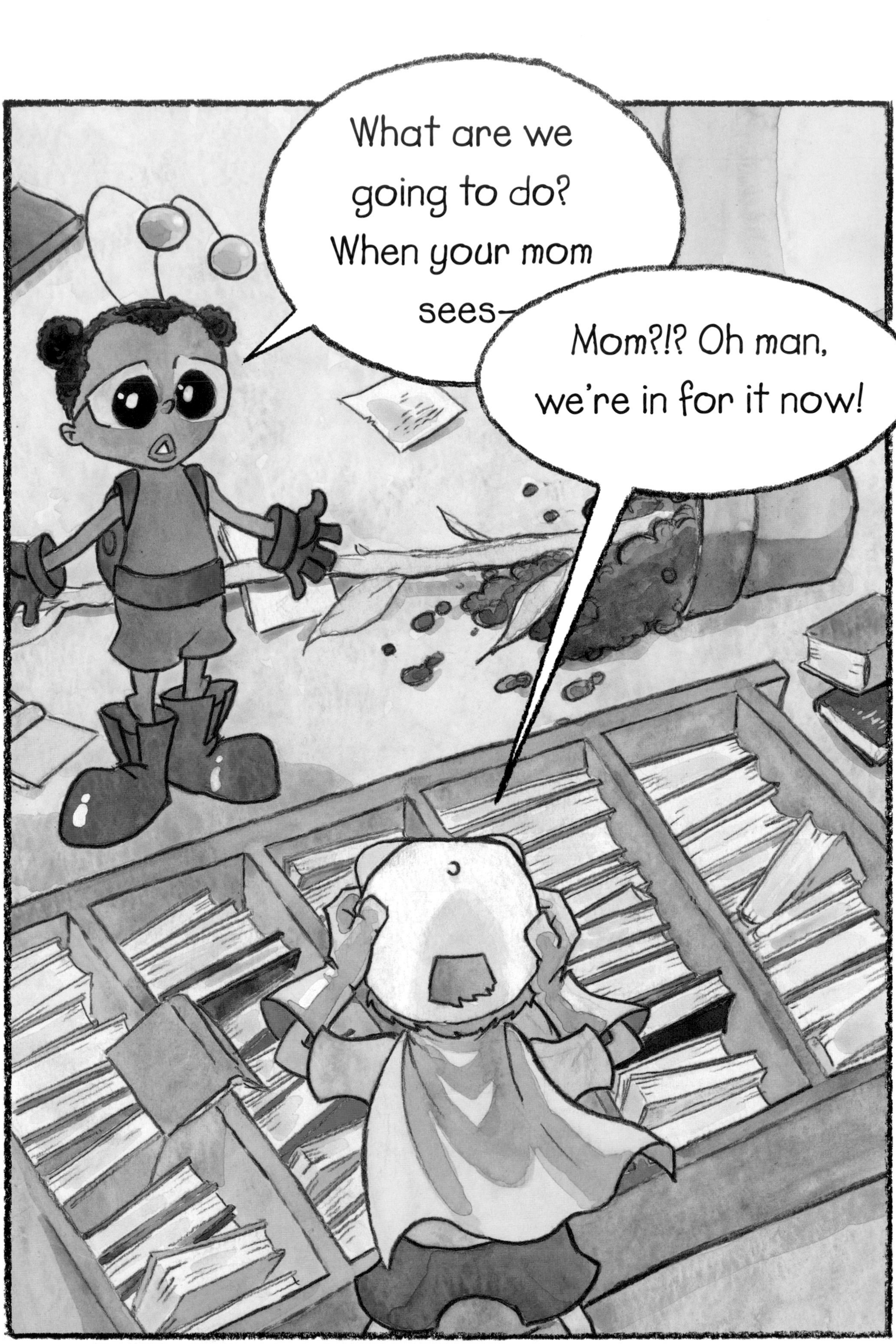
What are we going to do? When your mom sees—
Mom?!? Oh man, we're in for it now!

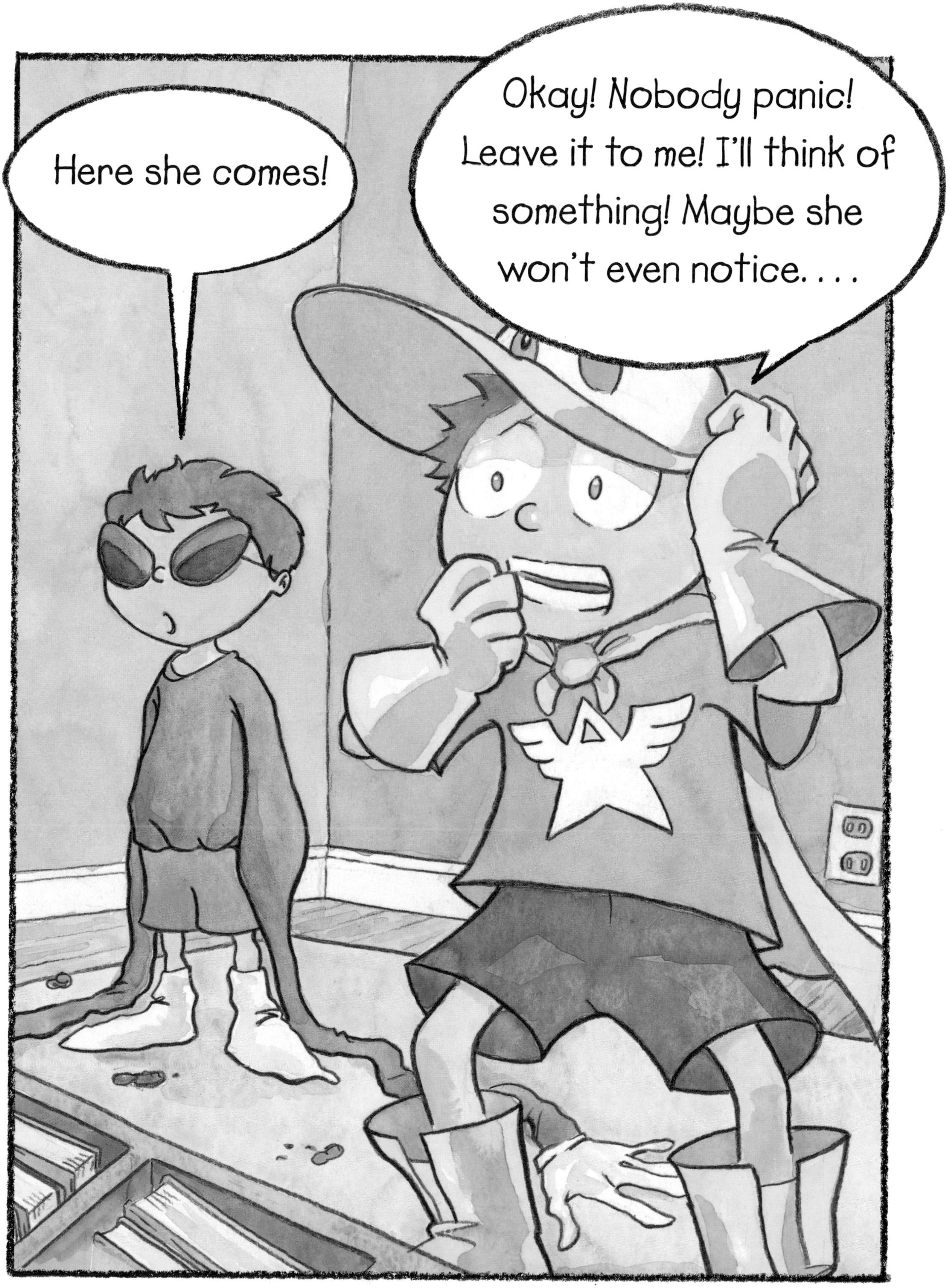
Here she comes!
Okay! Nobody panic! Leave it to me! I'll think of something! Maybe she won't even notice. . . .

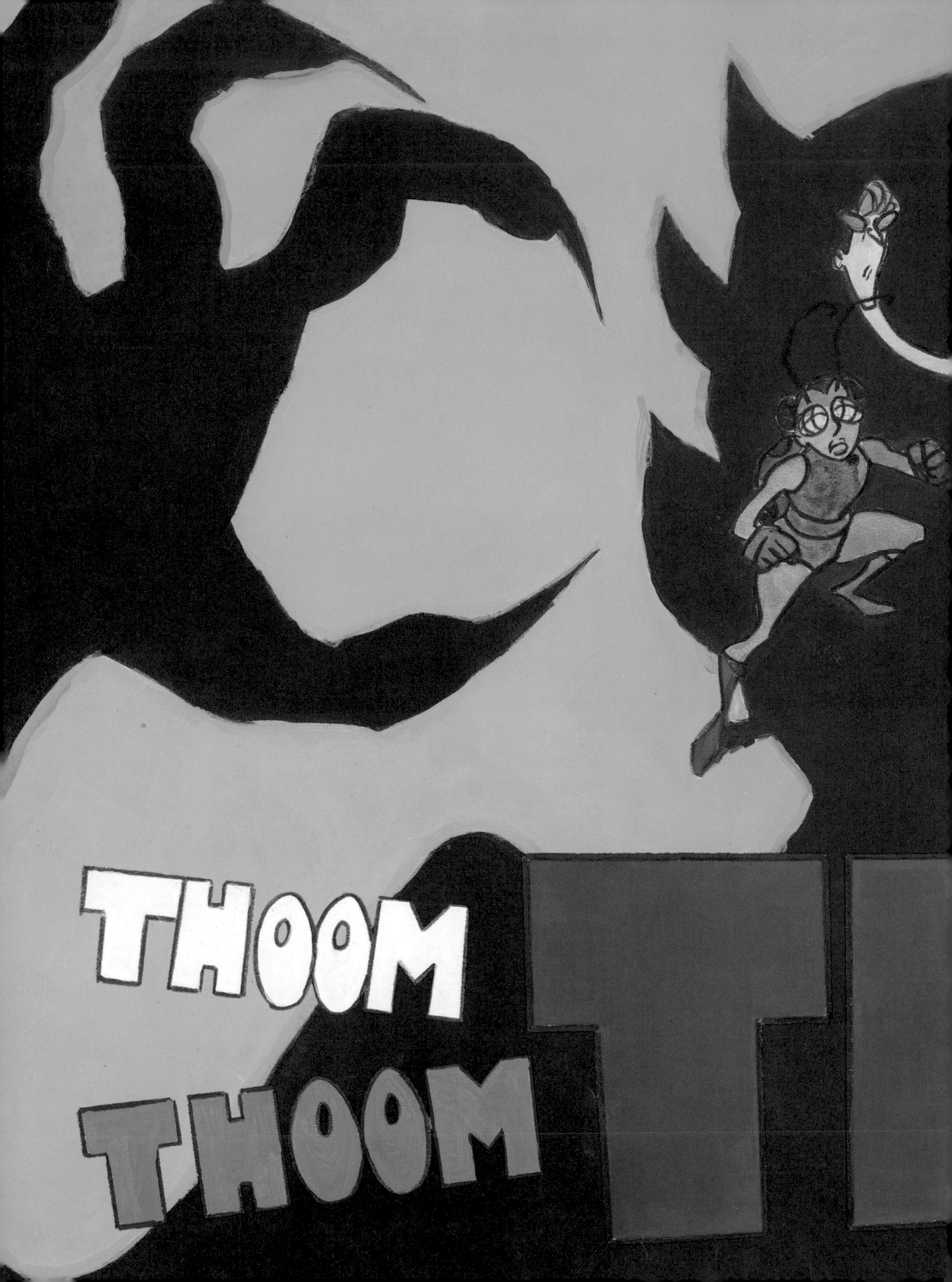
THOOM
THOOM

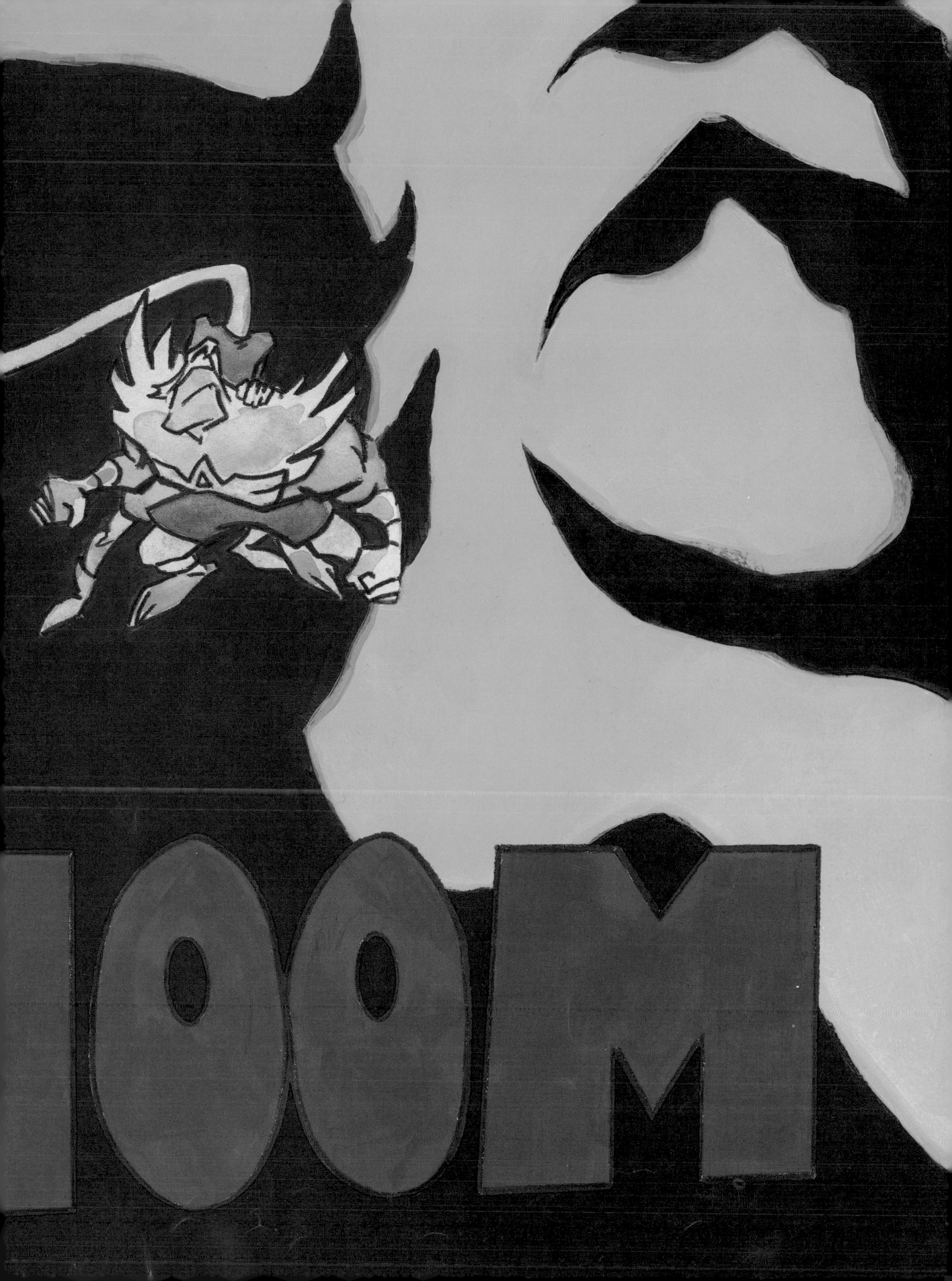

100M

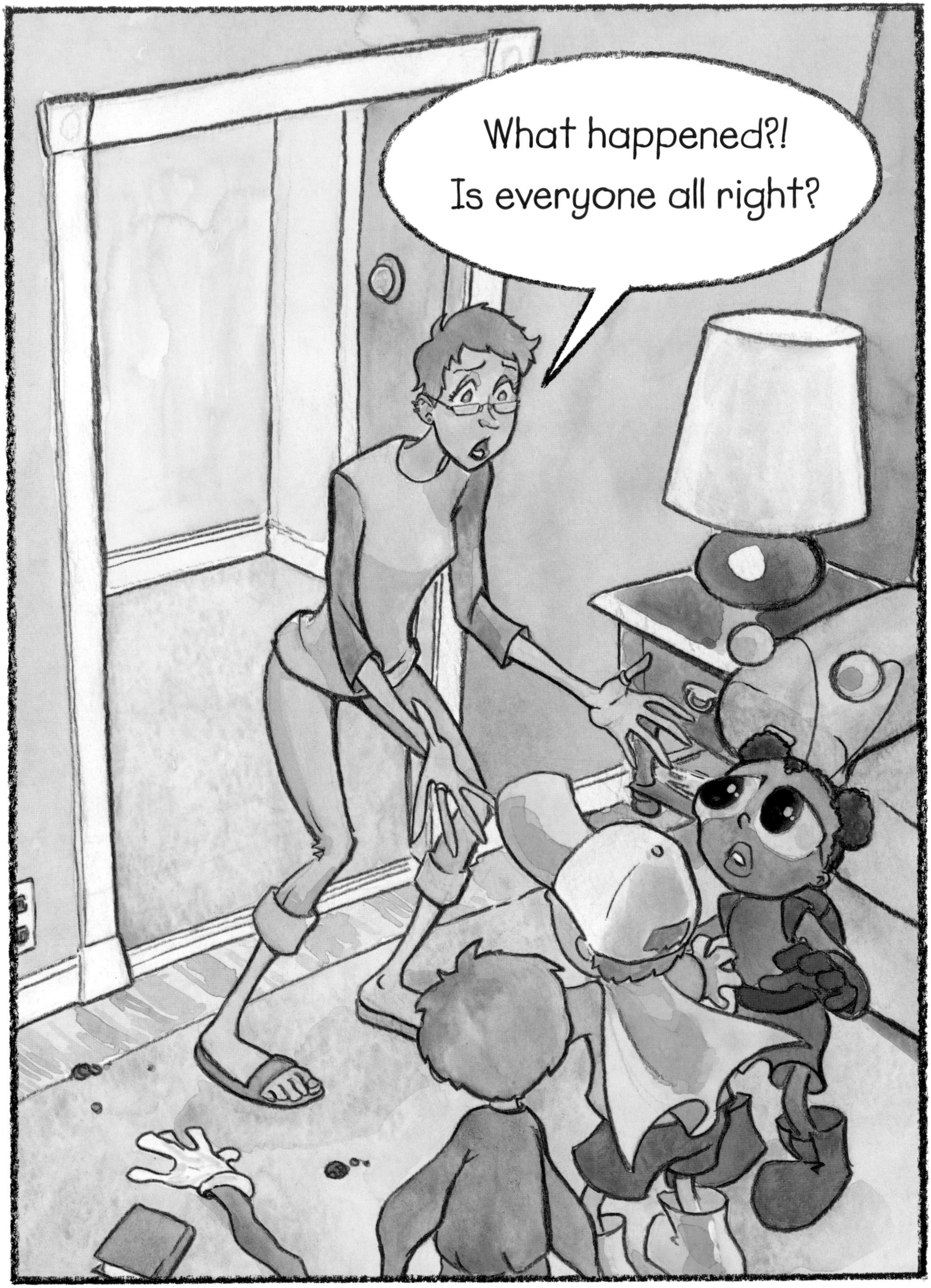
What happened?! Is everyone all right?

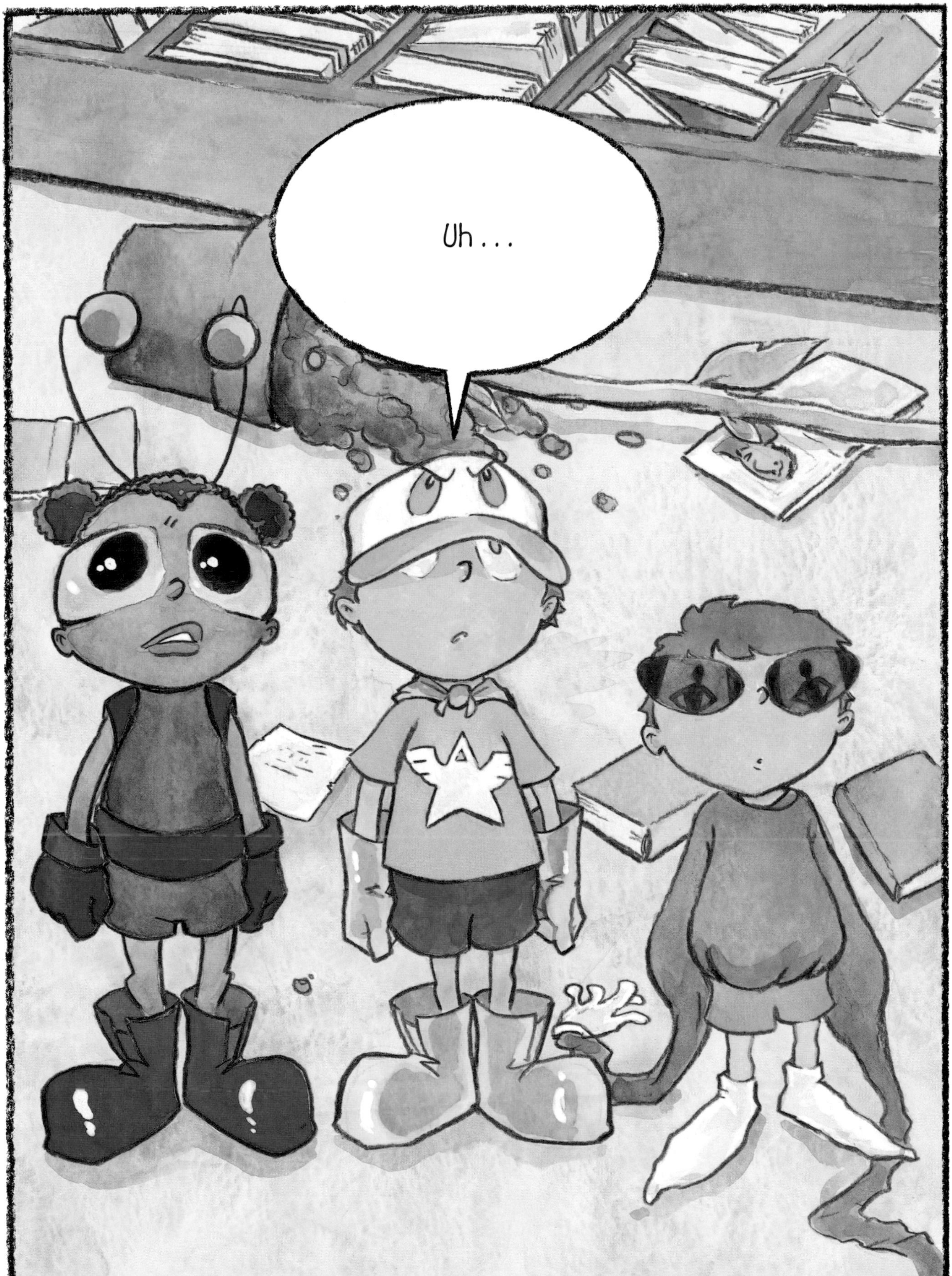
Uh . . .

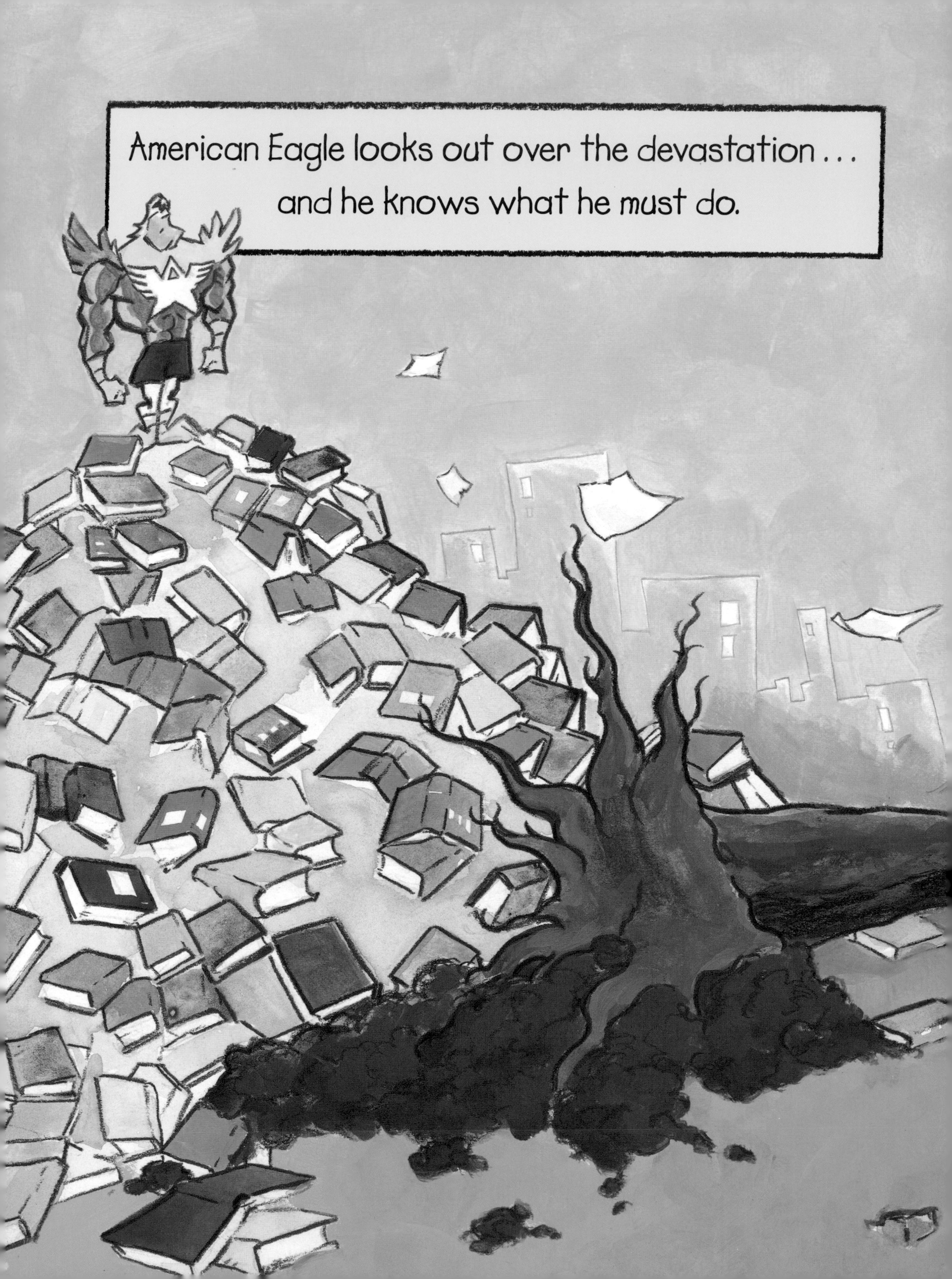
American Eagle looks out over the devastation . . .
. . . and he knows what he must do.

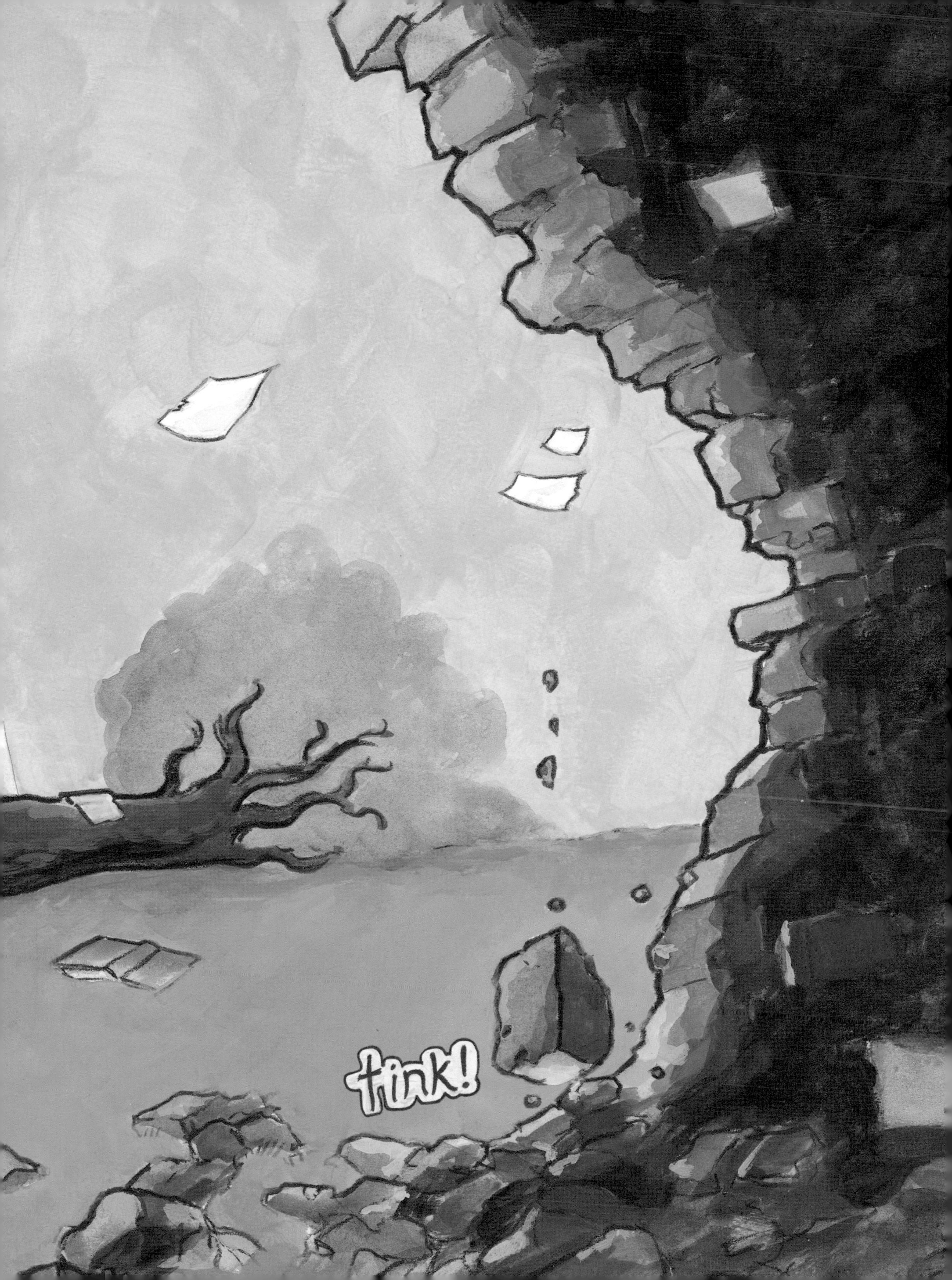
tink!

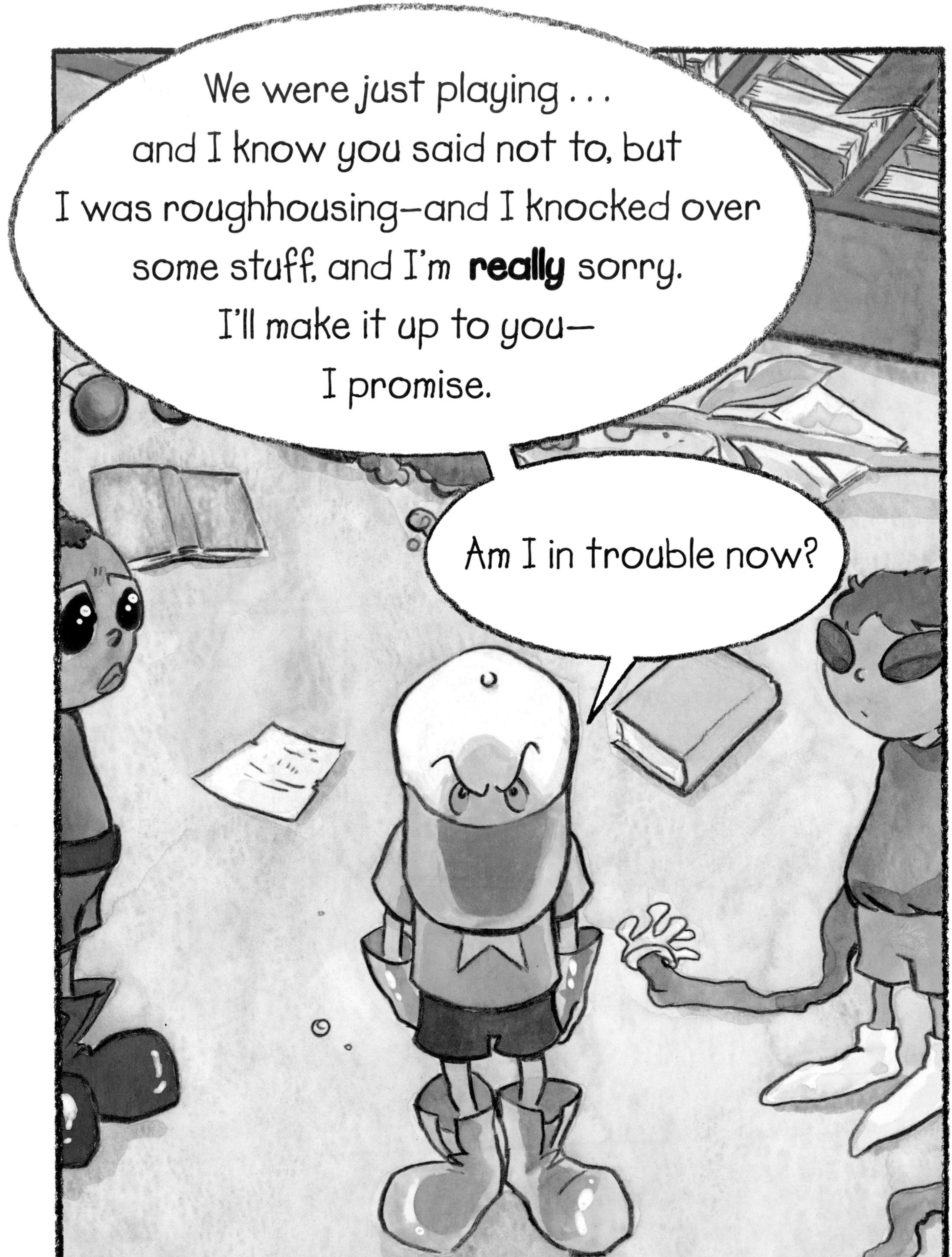
We were just playing . . .
and I know you said not to, but
I was roughhousing—and I knocked over
some stuff, and I'm **really** sorry.
I'll make it up to you—
I promise.
Am I in trouble now?

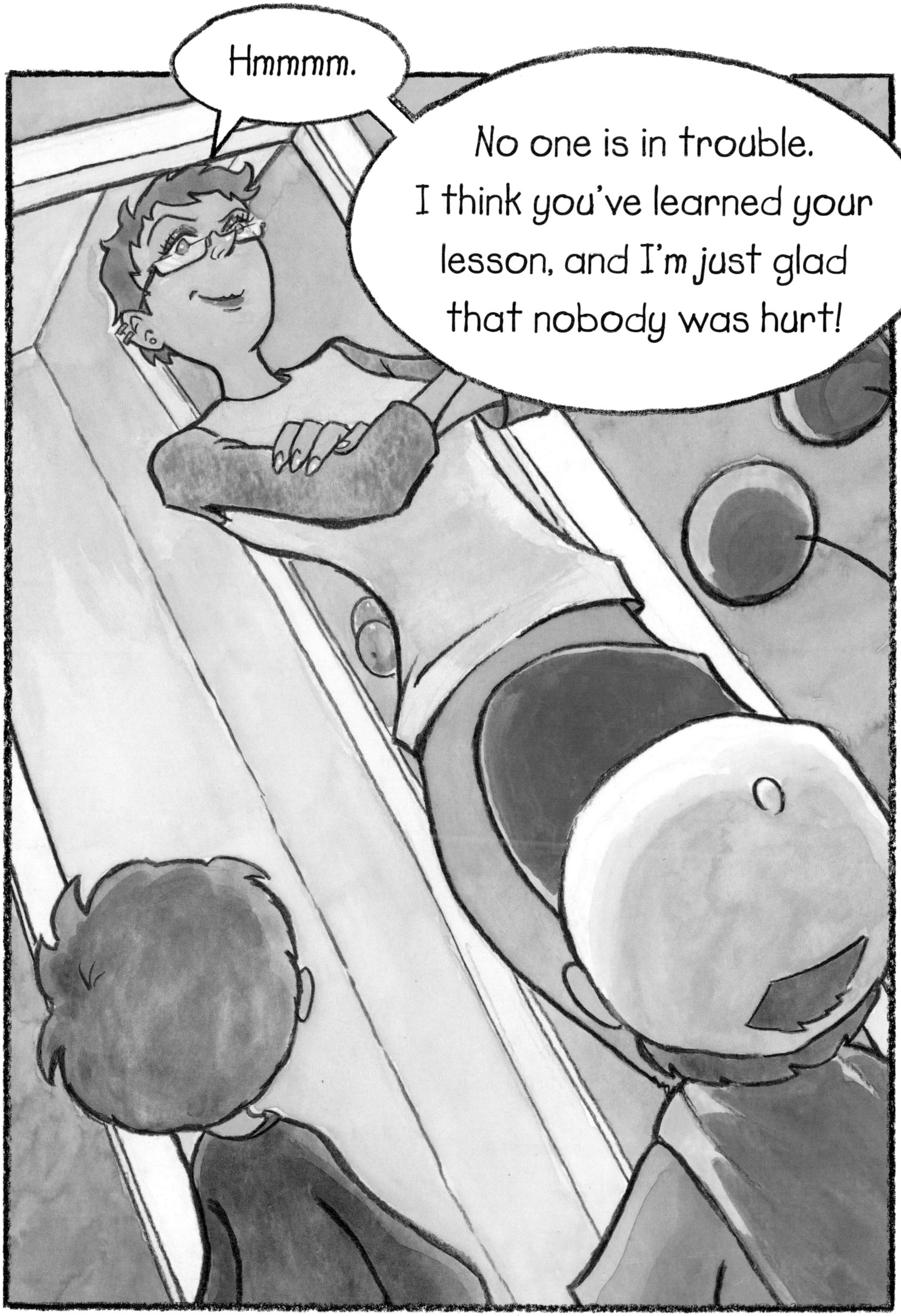
Hmmmm.
No one is in trouble. I think you've learned your lesson, and I'm just glad that nobody was hurt!

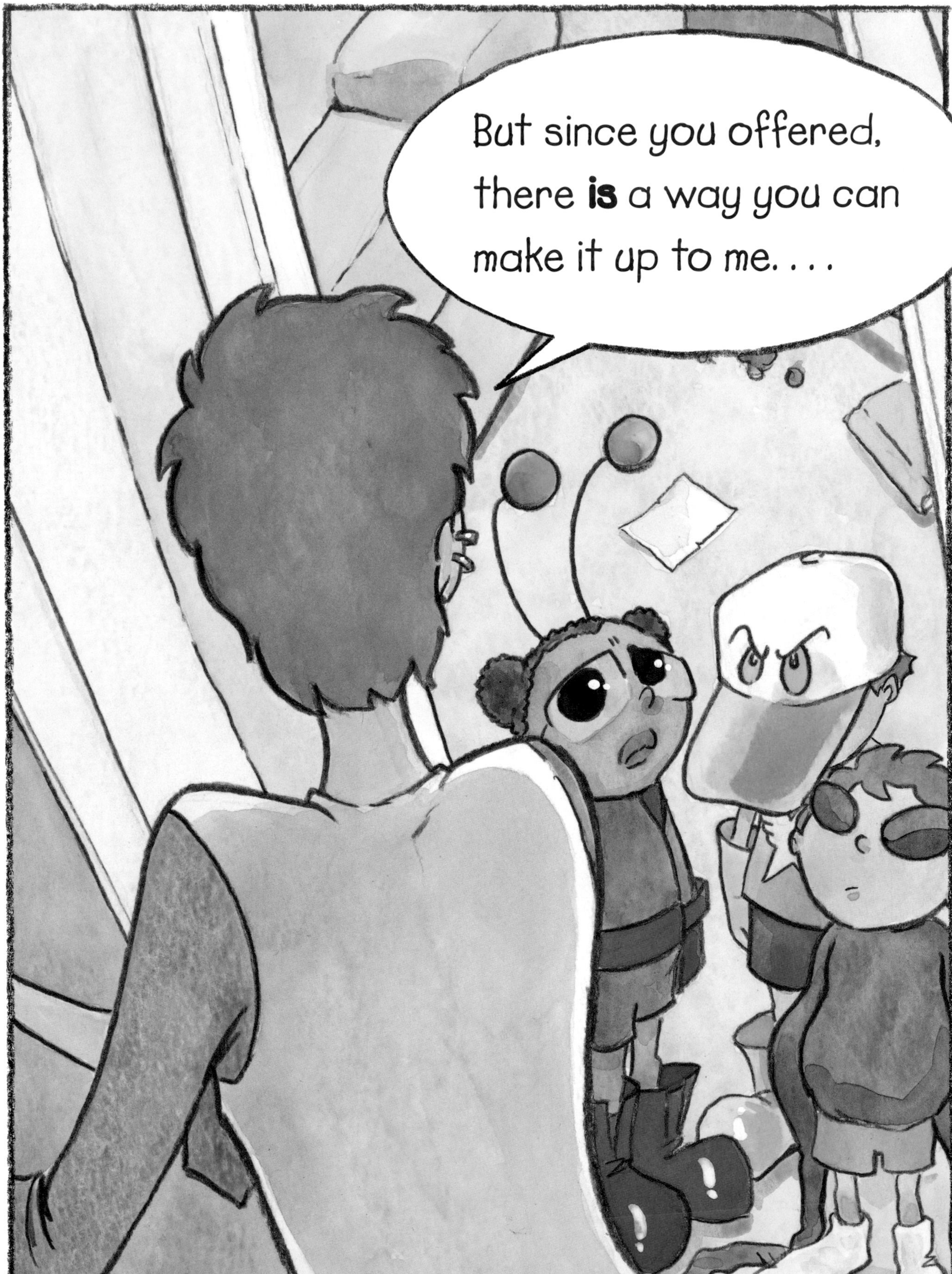
But since you offered, there **is** a way you can make it up to me. . . .

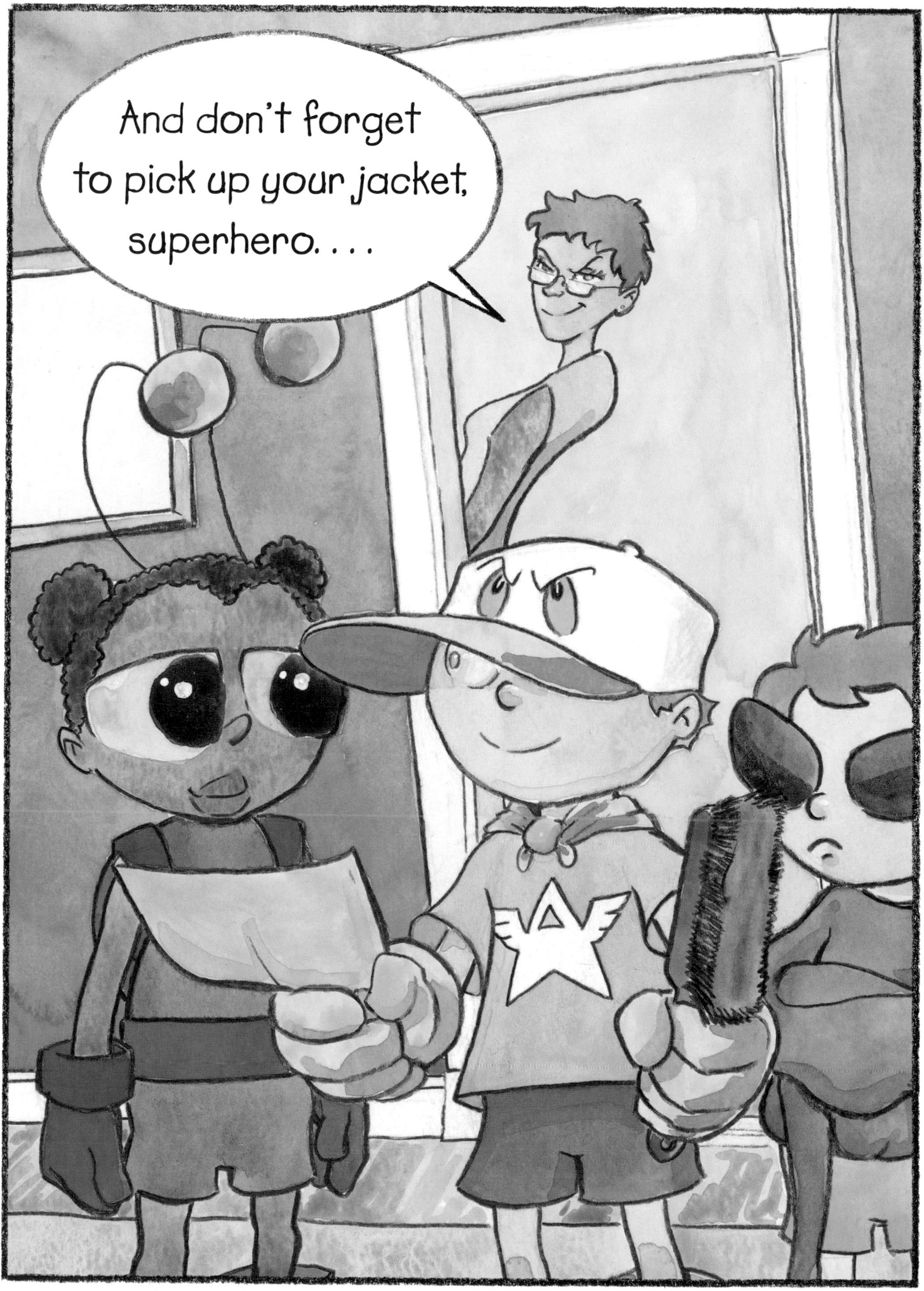
And don't forget to pick up your jacket, superhero. . . .

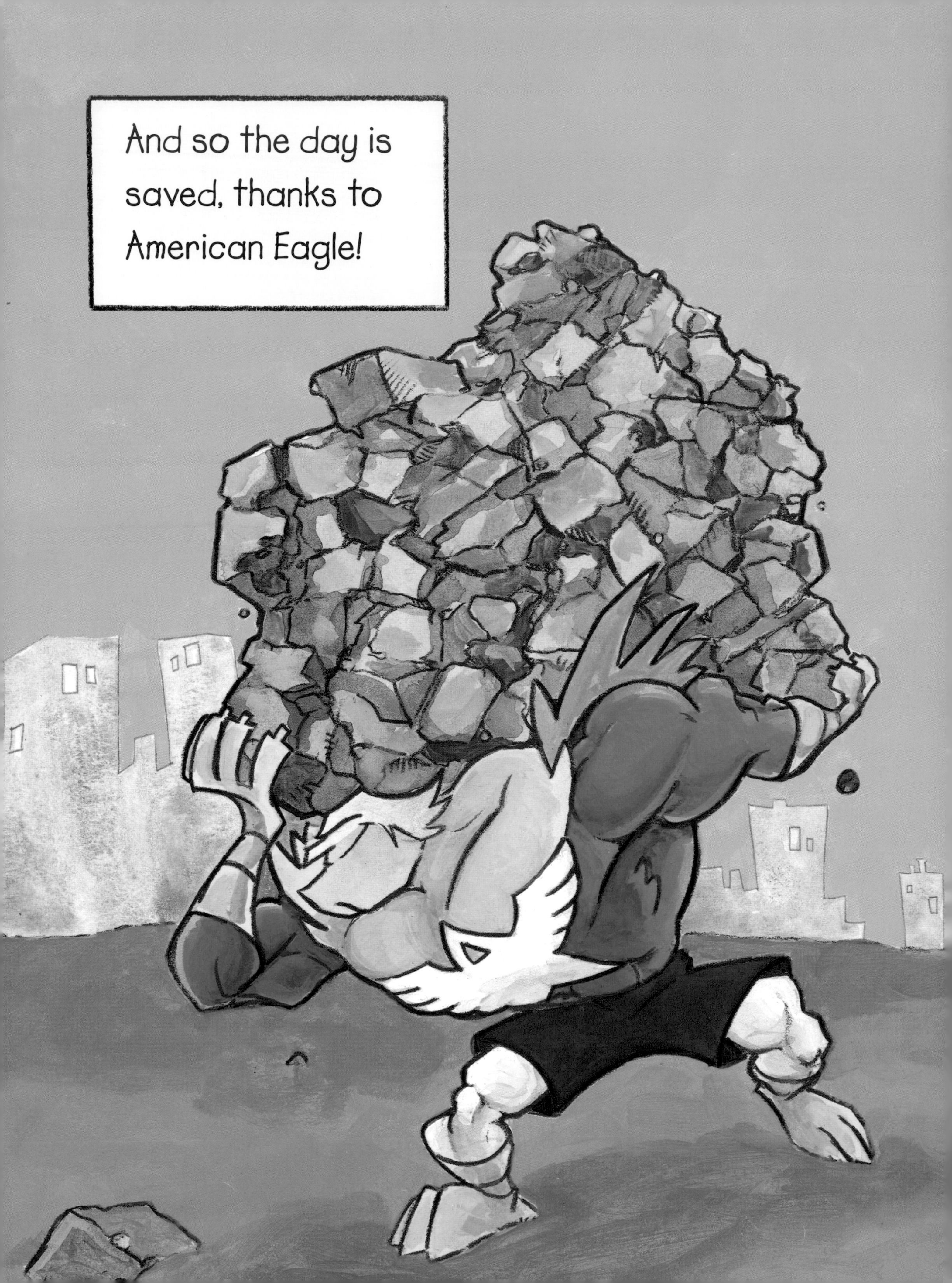
And so the day is saved, thanks to American Eagle!

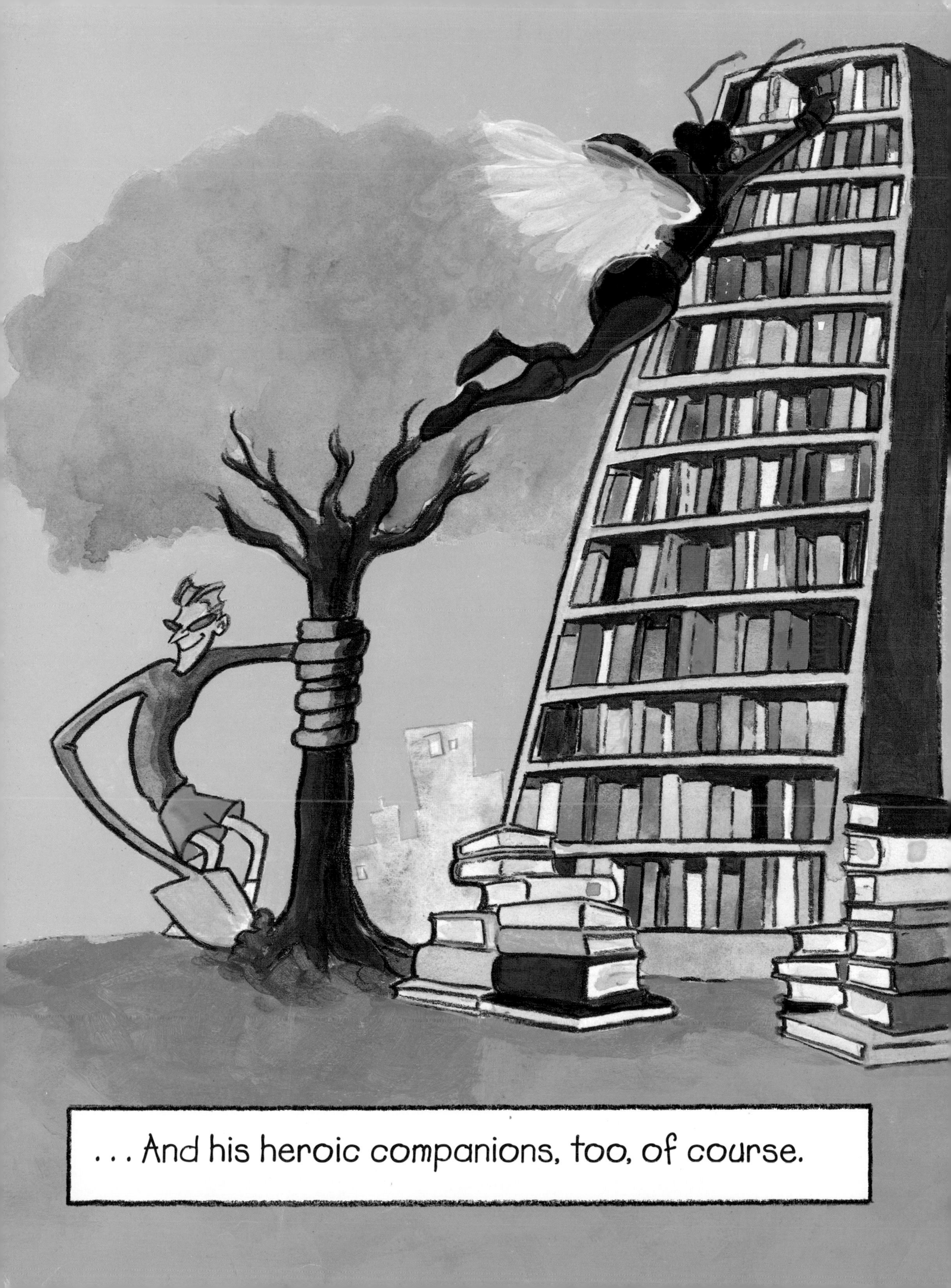
. . . And his heroic companions, too, of course.

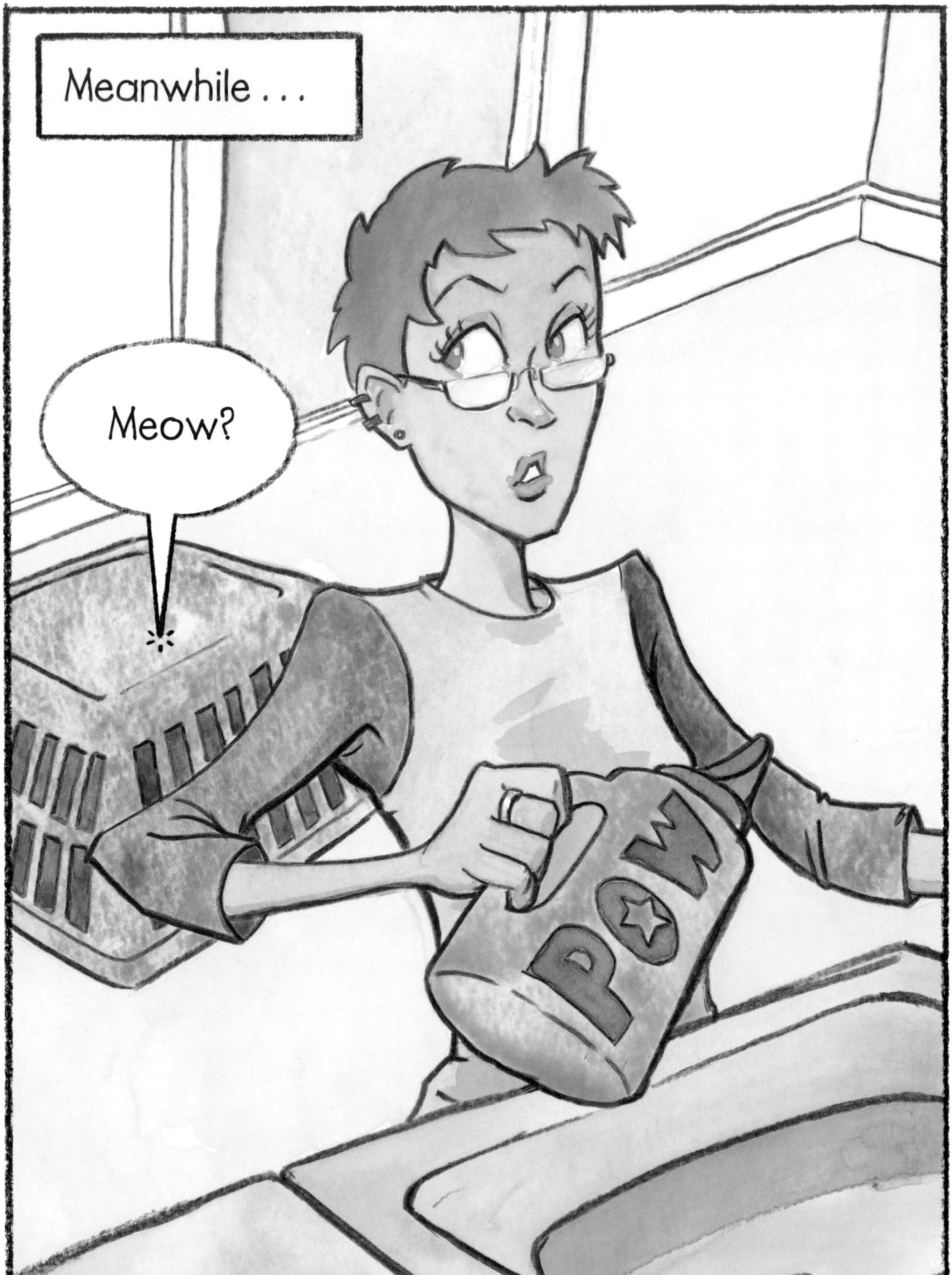
Meanwhile . . .
Meow?
POW